A Heart Realigned

by Elizabeth Maddrey

www.ElizabethMaddrey.com

Scripture quoted by permission. Quotations designated (NIV) are from THE HOLY BIBLE: NEW INTERNATIONAL VERSION®. NIV®. Copyright © 1973, 1978, 1984 by Biblica. All rights reserved worldwide.

Cover design by Jennifer Zemanek of Seedlings Design Studio

Published in the United States of America by Elizabeth Maddrey
www.ElizabethMaddrey.com

Other Books by Elizabeth Maddrey

Faith Departed
Hope Deferred
Love Defined

Stand alone novellas
Kinsale Kisses: An Irish Romance
Luna Rosa (book 2 of A Tuscan Legacy Multi-Author)

Non-Fiction
A Walk in the Valley: Christian encouragement for your
journey through infertility

For the most recent listing of all my books, please visit
my website.

For Tim

Because I would know nothing about romance

but for you.

1

Azure Hewitt eased her pickup to a stop in front of the stone mansion and shifted into park. The view of the mountains drew her gaze away from the building and her fingers itched for a paintbrush. Soon enough. The interior painting she was scheduled to do here at Peacock Hill wouldn't take more than a month, barring problems, and the owner—what was her name?—well, whatever it was, she'd said Azure was welcome to stay as long as she wanted. With this view? That was liable to be a good bit of time.

She hopped down from the cab and patted the front of her Harbor Green 1952 Studebaker pickup as she strode to the steps and climbed them two at a time. The house was nice, too, for people who were into that kind of thing. Azure was good with her truck and trailer. Anything else was just trappings. She pounded a fist on the door and tucked her hands into the pockets of her denim overalls. She'd covered this pair with paintings of horses running through the waves. The time she'd spent on Chincoteague Island had been inspirational. Then again, she could find inspiration wherever she was. Anyone could, if they took the time to look.

A petite blonde opened the door. A long second passed before her face morphed into a polite smile. "Can I help you?"

"Hope so. I'm Azure. I was hired to do some painting?" This wasn't the worst reception she'd ever gotten, but it was up there. Had she gotten the date wrong? "I thought I was supposed to start the day after Labor Day. On my calendar, that's today?"

"Of course. Sorry." The woman opened the door wider. "It's been a little crazy around here. I'm Deidre McIntyre."

Azure gave Deidre's hand a firm shake. "Nice to meet you in person."

"Come on in, I'll show you around. You can choose pretty much whichever room you want upstairs, well, on the second floor. My brother's bunking on three, and it's probably better not to make things too co-ed."

"I'm good." Azure pointed to the trailer hitched to her truck. "If there's a place I can unhook, I'll be set."

Deidre's eyebrows lifted. "A camping trailer?"

"Converted into a tiny house. It's got everything I need. Just let me know where's okay to set up. But you can show me around where I'll be painting, if you want." Maybe taking this job had been a bad idea, after all. Her parents had been opposed. If anything, that had pushed her to accept. Besides, it wasn't as if paying jobs like this came around all that often. She made ends meet mainly by keeping her expenses low and selling an occasional painting on the street in between the few of her works that galleries could move. "I can get started this afternoon."

"Tomorrow's fine. You must be exhausted after your drive." Deidre led Azure through the large entry hall, then to the right into an elegant, completely wood-paneled room. "The kitchen's just through those doors, you're welcome to use it if you change your mind about the trailer. This'll be the more formal dining room eventually and just over here is the breakfast room, where you'll do the bulk of your painting."

Azure nodded and surveyed the space. The room was a skinny rectangle, with a bay window on one short end and the archway into the dining room opposite. The two long walls were smooth and unadorned. "The pictures you sent me are what you want?"

"They are. I have more, too, if you need. I took a ton of them before repairing and ultimately repainting all of the plaster. It wasn't in good enough shape to salvage. But I'd like to recreate what was here as closely as we can."

"That shouldn't be a problem." Boring, maybe, but who was she to judge? It was like her father had said, if she took a job for someone else, she had to do what her employer asked. It wasn't an exact quote, he'd said something about being a slave and a few other choice words, but the gist was the same. "Printouts?"

"Oh. Sure. Is that better than email?"

"If they're printed, I can keep them close while I'm working. It's not really a good idea to have electronics around all the paint."

"That makes sense. If you want to come downstairs, we have the basics of a business center set up. I can print them for you now."

Azure shrugged. If she wasn't going to start painting right away, she had nothing but time. As they crossed the large entry again, the colorful stained-glass window at the landing of the stairs caught her eye. An enormous peacock took center stage, with smaller versions in the corners among decorative Art Deco embellishments. "I guess I see why it's called Peacock Hill."

Deidre laughed. "There's really no getting around it. You'll find peacocks everywhere if you look."

The front door swung open and a tall, handsome in a boy-next-door sort of way, man stomped his feet on the mat before entering. His eyes arrowed to Deidre and Azure could practically feel the heat between them. He grinned and jerked his head toward the front of the house. "Hey, babe. Where'd the sweet truck out front come from?"

Azure raised her hand. "It's mine."

Deidre reversed direction and met the man in the middle of the hall. They exchanged a brief hug before she turned, her arm still around his waist. "Jeremiah, this is Azure Hewitt, she's the painter I mentioned? Azure, this is my fiancé, Jeremiah Crawford."

"Nice to meet you." Jeremiah extended his hand. "You can sing the song if you need to, nearly everyone does. I figure it's better to embrace it than be constantly annoyed. I need to get Matt up here to see your truck."

"You don't want me to sing, trust me." Azure grinned. "But the truck'll be here as long as I am, so he's welcome to have a peek. Vintage car buff?"

"Of sorts. He and his uncle have been restoring a sixty-seven Stingray for the last five years or so. Matt runs the garage in town now that his uncle's retired."

A Stingray. Cliché man car. Still, to each his own, if this Matt person was doing the restoration, they might have something in common. "My dad and I spent about six years putting the truck back together. Got it for three hundred bucks from a farmer in—where were we?— Kansas, maybe? Worth it, in the long run, even though Dad griped about hauling it around with us until it could run on its own."

"Let's get you those pictures. Then, if you're sure about staying in the camper, you're welcome to set up wherever you'd like. If you prefer a little privacy, you can take the driveway around the back toward the lake and you'll see a bonfire area. It's a nice spot."

Privacy sounded like just the thing, and if she wasn't starting the work inside today, maybe she could set up her easel and take a whack at the view. "Great."

The stairs to the basement were considerably less grand than the main staircase that led up, but they were still glossy, dark wood that looked well cared for. The basement itself consisted of a short hall with three doors.

"This is the business center." Deidre pulled open the glass door and gestured for Azure to go in. "The other doors lead to apartments. Mine—well, I'll share it with Jeremiah once we're married—and my sister,

Claire's. She'll be managing the business side of things when we get up and running, hopefully in the spring. For now she's helping some with the renovations and getting the website up."

"Okay." There was no way Azure was going to remember all this. Nor did she particularly care. She was here to paint, not make friends. She'd move on again when the job was done and she'd satisfied her need to paint the view.

Deidre tapped at one of the computers on the sleek, black desk. "You're welcome to use the Internet down here if you want. Login information is on the desk by each machine."

"Thanks. I don't do a lot online, so my phone's usually fine. But I'll keep it in mind."

The printer whirred to life and paper started to shoot out the top. When it stopped, Deidre collected the stack, tapped it on the desk, and handed it to Azure. "There you go. We're all pretty early risers, so whenever you want to get started, just come on in. Do you need supplies, or money to get them?"

"I'm probably okay. I'll let you know if that changes." Azure flipped through the photos, pausing as the pictures changed from the breakfast room to a painting over a fireplace. "Did you need me to do this one, too?"

Deidre peered at the paper and frowned. "Maybe you could take a look at it. I feel like it just needs some touchups—same for the murals on the ceilings—but if you think it's better to start fresh, we can talk about that."

Azure nodded. "Let's start with the breakfast room and go from there."

"That works. I appreciate your willingness to come all this way. And if you change your mind about staying in the house, there's plenty of room on the second floor. Right now it's just Anna Hamilton, one of the landscapers and my brother's fiancée, up there."

"Everyone here engaged?" She was going to be tripping over lovebirds everywhere she looked. Great.

Deidre laughed. "Feels like it, but no. Claire isn't. And Jeremiah brings his guy friends around often enough that it shouldn't feel too much like couple central."

Azure nodded. She didn't plan to spend much time hanging out. She was here to paint, that was it. She waved the printouts in a mock salute and turned toward the stairs. "I'm going to go get settled. You have my cell number if you need me, right?"

"I do. We'd love to have you join us for dinner, if you're in the mood for company."

"Thanks. I'll let you know."

Azure stepped down from the trailer and tucked the key into her pocket. She'd found the clearing past the lake just like Deidre had promised and it was perfect. She had a magnificent view of the mountains and, more important than anything else, privacy. She'd parked her trailer in a bit of shade and unhitched it from the truck. She'd told Deidre she was good on supplies, but one look at the drawers in the kitchen had made it clear she needed to buy some groceries.

So much for getting a start on the painting of the mountains that was already an itch at the base of her spine.

She could eat dinner with the people at the house—would it be everyone Deidre had named? But that would only handle dinner. When breakfast rolled around, she'd be in the same predicament. Maybe a worse one, as she was completely out of coffee. No. Better to head into town and grab some essentials. Maybe stop by the hardware store she'd noticed and poke around as well. There were probably some interesting finds in there. Small town shops like that always had something unique.

She climbed into the cab of her truck and, with a last look over her shoulder at the trailer, and the view, turned the key. The engine roared to life before settling into its constant rumble. Azure smiled. Modern vehicles might be quieter and have a smoother ride, but her truck was a gem and she wouldn't trade it for the world.

She eased into drive and bumped along the dirt and gravel driveway that led around the lake and back to the house before merging with the winding mountain road that would take her into town.

Town, such as it was, had a row of buildings on the main street—not in fact *called* Main Street—and a sprinkle of other businesses on the blocks leading in. She'd passed a huge, modern grocery store on her way from the highway into town, but a quick search had revealed a family-owned one here in the main area.

She pulled her truck to a spot at the curb a few stores down from the green and white striped awning that hung over a rolling wooden display of fruit. Azure didn't miss the curious glances of passersby as she walked, hands tucked in the pockets of her hand-painted overalls, toward the grocery store. It was a small town. Everyone knew everybody else. Or at least recognized them. With her unfashionably long hair and clothing choices, she probably stuck out more than most, though. She was used to that, too.

The fruit out front was buffed and shined to perfection. The owner obviously took pride in his or her wares and clearly had local support.Mom and Pop shops like this rarely stayed in business up against the kinds of chains like the big supermarket by the highway. Azure picked up a hand basket and carefully selected three of the oranges from the display before entering.

It smelled like cookies.

Azure couldn't stop her smile. She sniffed, turning her head until she caught a stronger whiff of the chocolate and sugar scent. She headed in that direction first. Cookies might not have been on her mental list, but if they were going to bake them, she ought to do them the courtesy of eating a few.

After collecting a paper bag of warm chocolate chip cookies, she browsed the aisles, grabbing a few items here and there, before meandering to the register.

"Did you find everything okay?" The matronly woman stationed at the check-out smiled as she punched each item into the register by hand. No fancy scanners here, but at least the machines were electric. Azure had half expected to see big push buttons and an enter key that said *cha-ching* when pressed.

"I did. You have a lovely store."

"Thank you." The woman angled her head as she dropped the oranges on a small scale. "You just passing through?"

"I'm painting some murals up at Peacock Hill. Probably be in town a month. Maybe longer." Azure reached into her pocket for her zippered pouch where she kept her cash.

"Really? Word is that Yankee girl is doing a bang-up job getting the old place back together. Hope she lets all the rest of us get a look see before she opens it up for weddings and the like. That old house is the reason the town's here." The woman entered the last item and told Azure the total. "Did you need a bag?"

"Oh. No." Azure pulled out the money and offered it. When she'd zipped the pouch back up and tucked it into her pocket, she removed a folded square of cloth, unlatched the Velcro band around it, and shook it open. "I always have one of these with me."

The cashier smiled and rubbed the material between her fingers. "Feels like a t-shirt."

"Used to be one. I just sewed the bottom together and cut off the arms, widened the neck opening, then add a strip of Velcro for folding." Azure loaded her groceries into the bag and accepted her change. "Thanks."

"Have a nice day, now."

Azure smiled. Exiting the store, she turned right, away from her truck, and walked to the end of the building. A small alley led between the grocery and the shop next door. She ambled down the immaculate space to the end and peeked around the corner, her smile morphing into a grin when her gaze landed on the dumpster.

She set the t-shirt bag down by the wall and pried open the lid, sniffing. Not too bad. Azure hoisted herself up and crawled over the lip, pushing aside an empty box to unearth a carton of shredded cheese. It was still cool. The date stamped on the package was yesterday. Azure shook her head and dropped the cheese into the empty box. It'd still be good for a week.

She picked through the top level of the trash, stopping when she reached a box that was clearly past its prime. Good enough. Azure hoisted the box she'd filled with her gleanings over the edge of the dumpster and, leaning over the edge, lowered it so it was just a short drop to the ground. She glanced back at the trash, shuffled it around a little so it was more evenly distributed like it had been when she arrived, and then levered herself up and out of the container.

Azure brushed debris off her overalls, hefted her box, grabbed her bag of purchased items, and strode back between the buildings. Hunger was no longer going to be an issue. The dozen-and-a-half eggs she'd found under the cheese were a real find. They'd still been cold as well. She must have just missed whoever did the stock disposal. She'd keep that in mind.

A man squatted beside her truck, his head angled as he tried to peer under the front. Azure set her groceries in the back and cleared her throat. "Can I help you?"

He stood, his green eyes bright, and extended his hand. "I'm Matt. Just admiring your truck. And seeing as I doubt there are two of these beauties in town, you have to be, Cyan was it?"

She laughed and shook his hand. "Close. Azure."

"Same color family, at least."

"My brother would beg to differ. He's always felt cyan was more green than blue."

Matt frowned. "You argue about colors?"

"Well, it's his name. He didn't want us both to be shades of blue." She shrugged. "He doesn't like it that I'm older than he is, so he likes to be difficult. Want me to open the hood?"

"I really do. But you have groceries. They probably need to get back in the fridge?"

"It'd be better. You busy?"

He shook his head.

"Why don't you come on up? I was planning on making hot dogs and potato salad. You can drool over the engine while I fix supper."

"Just like that?"

"Sure. I'm reasonably certain if you were some kind of serial killer Deidre's boyfriend—fiancé, whatever—wouldn't have mentioned that you'd love to see the truck. Add to that, I've got more hot dogs than I can probably eat tonight, so why let them go to waste?" She cocked her head to the side. He was tall, lean, and handsome. Her heart gave a little flutter. Oh yeah, if he was going to be around much, hanging out at Peacock Hill might be even more interesting. "Want a ride?"

2

Matt swallowed. The invitation in Azure's eyes was obvious. His cheeks heated. She didn't look like a woman who chewed up men and spit them out, not in dirty overalls with her long black hair in a braid coiled around her head, but suddenly a little caution seemed like it might be advised. "I need to make a stop. I'll meet you up there in say forty?"

"Sure." She grinned. "If you want to drink something other than water, you'll want to bring it with you. I'm set up back near what looks like a bonfire spot."

"You're not staying in the house?"

Azure shook her head and tugged open the truck door. "Nope. See ya."

The engine roared to life before she pulled smoothly away from the curb and down the street.

Matt blew out a breath. "Wow."

It had been a while since a woman had caught his eye. Azure—had she said her last name? He mentally scrolled through their conversation. Nope. Then again, had he? Probably not. He'd been too busy trying to gather up his scattered thoughts. The truck by itself was a thing of beauty, but it paled in comparison to its driver.

Shaking his head, he tugged his phone from his pocket and began to walk back down the block toward his garage. His uncle had come in today, so he'd had a little more flexibility than usual. The two other part-time employees worked harder for their old boss than they ever did for Matt. Maybe in another thirty years they'd finally accept that he was in charge.

Thirty years.

Matt was saved from a depressing reel of the future stretched out like an unending exercise in monotony by his friend's voice on the phone.

"Hey, Matt. You find the truck?"

"I did. You failed to mention the woman that went with it."

Jeremiah laughed. "No. I said the painter drove it. Pretty sure I mentioned she was a she."

Had he? "That wasn't nearly enough information."

"What do you mean?" There was a pause. "Oh. Really? She is absolutely not who I imagined you going for. Did you catch the hair?"

Glossy and black, it had been wrapped around her head in a braid, like a crown. It only added to her appeal. What would it be like to run his fingers through? "Yeah? So? I've been known to appreciate a braid."

"Seriously? It's gotta reach her hips when it's down, man. Did you pay any attention to how thick that braid was?"

"Apparently not," Matt muttered. Didn't matter. Long hair wasn't a deal breaker. Just because he tended to go for girls with short and sassy hair didn't mean he couldn't branch out. "Why are you fixated on her hair? You've got a woman. I'm pretty sure she has her own hair."

"That she does. I'm just surprised. I never would've picked Azure for you. I mean, come on, her name is a color."

"So is her brother's. Apparently." He winced and, with a glance into the garage bay where both of his mechanics were huddled under the hood of a car, turned toward the office. Maybe Jeremiah was right. He was entirely too interested for a, what, three-minute conversation on the street? "We're having dinner tonight."

"You and her brother?"

"Ha ha. Me and Azure."

"How'd that happen? Last time you asked a girl out, you'd known her for more than six months. I've known turtles who move faster than you do."

"Whatever."

"I'm serious, man. I need the details."

Heat crawled up his neck. Matt peered around the office door to double-check his uncle wasn't inside. "She asked me."

Matt held the phone away from his ear to save his hearing from Jeremiah's laughter. He let it go on for a minute before interrupting. "You about done?"

Jeremiah muffled another laugh, turning it into a snorting snicker. "Yeah. Think so." He cleared his throat. "So. This ought to be fun."

"Dinner? Yeah, probably. She said she'd let me check out the truck in more detail."

"No, man, not dinner. You and Azure. I'm gonna get a kick out of watching you fall."

Fall? Like in love? Matt snorted before he could catch himself. Maybe he and Azure would have some laughs, hang out. But he'd realized a long time ago that he didn't have what it took to fall in love. In any part of his life. "Whatever. But if you're going to be up at the Hill, maybe I'll swing by the main house on my way out. Then I can punch you in person."

"I'd like to see you try." Jeremiah drew in a breath. "Look, Matt. Deidre does basic background on anyone she hires, so this girl's probably not a serial killer or anything, but the fact of the matter is, we don't know much about her. So be careful, okay?"

"Sure. Look, I gotta go." His uncle appeared in the doorway of the office with two cups of coffee as Matt ended the call. Careful. It was hot dogs and an engine. How dangerous could that be?

It was closer to an hour by the time Matt made it to Peacock Hill. He glanced at the cars parked by the cedars in front of the house. Looked like Jeremiah had talked Danny into swinging by, too. No doubt the two of them would try to be cute and make more comments about him and the new girl. They should both know better.

The driveway turned into bouncy ruts once he passed the house and started curving around the lake. He really should mention that to Deidre. If she was planning to open in the spring, she was going to need better access for anyone who wanted to visit. He caught a glimpse of the teal of Azure's truck and smiled. Not many people would've bothered to try and match the paint color to one of the selections Studebaker offered. It was a nice bit of attention to detail. Was she like that in all aspects of her life?

He parked his truck next to hers and climbed down. There was a small campfire going outside an aqua and white vintage trailer. She'd rigged a grill over the flames and had hot dogs arranged on the top. Foil packets circled the fire on the ground.

Matt strode to the trailer door and knocked. "Azure?"

The door swung open. "Hey, you made it. I got everything going, but figured I'd do a little cooking ahead while I had the fire."

"Makes sense. But they'll let you use the kitchen in the house, I'm sure."

"Oh, I have a kitchen in here, too. I just would rather cook outside when I can. You want the tour?"

The tour? The trailer was maybe ten feet long and six feet wide. "Will we both even fit in there?"

She laughed and stepped back. "Come on in, all the comforts of home and then some."

Matt ducked under the door frame and entered. He could practically touch both sides of the trailer width-wise if he stretched out his arms. "So?"

"Kitchen, you can see, is there on your right."

He turned, eyebrows lifting. "A three burner stove?"

Azure chuckled. "Told you. All the comforts of home. Little fridge under the cook top. And this panel flips down to make an eating area. Or a desk, depending on what I'm doing. Plus there's lots of storage, as you see."

He nodded and eyed the bench. "Seating for one?"

"Sure. But I have a camp stool for company. Or we can sit outside. I have a folding table and four chairs that I set up when I'm parked for the night." Azure turned and gestured to the back of the trailer where a mattress on a platform ran the width of the space. "Bedroom. That's a double, in case you're wondering. And this little closet is a full bathroom—well, a shower and toilet. No tub, obviously."

"Obviously." He took in the tidy space and breathed in deeply. He'd never considered himself claustrophobic, but this was small. "It's nice?"

She grinned. "I think so. But of course, it's not for everyone. Let's go back outside, you're pale."

Pale. Whatever. Still, Matt stepped down out of the trailer and frowned. "So you live there while you're on jobs. What about when you aren't? Where's home?"

"You're looking at it."

His jaw dropped open. "But...your mail... and don't you have to have an address for things like a driver's license?"

"Sure. I keep a P.O. box, it has a street address." She shrugged. "I have a friend who collects the mail periodically and sends it on to wherever I am. If there's anything worth having."

How did someone live like that? No roots? Just, what? Driving from place to place as the whim struck? "No family? You mentioned a brother?"

Azure squatted by the fire, poked the hot dogs, and used tongs to pull them off the grill onto a plate. "Sure. Cyan. Plus another brother and two sisters. My parents had a school bus when we were all little. They've downgraded to something a little bigger than my own trailer now."

"A bus. You grew up on a bus with seven people?"

Her laugh was light, almost tinkling. "Sure. You spend a lot of time outside. And if you don't know any different, it's not so bad. Makes me appreciate having my own space now, certainly."

"I bet." Matt tried to wrap his mind around it. After his parents died, his aunt and uncle had raised him in their comfortable five-bedroom home. It had been the three of them, and even then sometimes he'd avoided going home because it was too crowded. "You really like it, don't you?"

"No point in doing something that you don't. Grab a chair, dinner's ready." Azure carried the hot dogs over to the square table with two chairs set up in the shade. "I made some iced tea or I have water."

"Tea sounds great, thanks. Can I get anything?"

"Nope. I've got it. You sit."

Matt pulled out a chair, frowning slightly and giving it a firm wiggle before gingerly lowering himself to it. He didn't consider himself a large man, but these things were relative when faced with a wooden chair that looked like it would collapse in a stiff breeze. He watched as Azure gathered the hot dogs, buns, and several bowls and brought them to the table. His mouth watered. "It smells good."

"Thanks. Dig in." Azure stabbed a hot dog with her fork and plopped it into a bun that was already on her plate.

Okay. Praying was clearly not high on her priority list. Feeling awkward, Matt bowed his head for a moment and sent up quick thanks for the food before reaching for his own hot dog.

"Grace. I always forget grace. Sorry." Azure scooped potato salad onto her plate and nudged the bowl toward Matt. "It's not that I don't pray, just so you know. I do. I'm just not as into the cultural things that don't really mean anything, you know?"

"I'm sorry?"

She picked up her hot dog. "Praying before a meal or as you get in the car, that sort of thing. I mean, that's just what you do, right? Doesn't really mean anything. So I don't see the point."

"Or it's taking a moment out of your day to be thankful for the food that God's seen fit to put in front of you. And asking for safety. Maybe I see how sometimes it feels like it's just a routine, but even if it is, what's wrong with routinely thanking God?" Matt bit into his hot dog. She had a knack with the grill, that was certain, and she attracted him like no woman had for a long time, but between the trailer and her thoughts on prayer, it was becoming clear that Azure wasn't the right woman for him. At all.

3

Azure clamped a thin paintbrush between her teeth as she dipped another into a blob of paint on her palette. She carefully stroked down the wing of the bluebird she was adding to the twist of ivy she'd added earlier. The ivy curled out from the corner of the room and would twine around to form a border just under the crown molding on all four walls. The work was intricate, but even with the oval mural in the center of the ceiling it shouldn't take more than a couple of weeks to finish the room.

"Looking good."

She turned and smiled, reaching for the brush in her mouth and starting down the stepladder. "Thanks."

"You don't have to stop on my account. I just thought I'd poke my head in." Deidre shrugged. "Mostly I was curious what it would look like."

"Hopefully like the pictures you gave me, but without the fading and cracks, right?" Azure set her supplies down on the floor and stretched her arms over her head. "It's a good time for a break. If I'm not careful,

I forget to drink water throughout the day and end up with muscle cramps."

"In that case, come on into the kitchen and sit for a few minutes. Did you get a chance to look at those other murals?"

Azure grabbed her thermos and followed the petite blonde who seemed to be a bundle of energy. "I did. I can touch them up, no problem. And I tend to agree with you that they don't need to be started fresh. I'm concerned about a couple of the colors—matching them might be tricky—but I'll do what I can and I doubt most people will notice."

Deidre slid onto a stool at the small table in the retro-styled kitchen and unscrewed the cap on a bottle of water. "That's great news. There's water in the fridge, help yourself."

"Tap okay?"

"Sure, if you want. It's a little bit of an acquired taste though."

Azure held her thermos under the faucet. "I'm sure it's fine. I'm used to the varieties in water. I'm almost to the point that it's fun to see what the taste will be. Almost. There's a place in, gosh, where was I? Georgia, maybe? Where there was a distinct sulfur taste to all the water. That took some getting used to."

Deidre shuddered. "I don't think I'd take the time to bother getting used to it."

Azure sipped. There was definitely some sort of taste to the water. What it was she couldn't put her finger on, but all things considered, it wasn't terrible. "What have you been working on? It all looks ready to go from what I've seen."

"Mostly finishing touches, to be honest. Today I fixed all the little cracks in the walls on the third floor so it's ready to paint. Well, it'll be ready to paint once I've sanded them down. The second floor's already good to go, so maybe we'll start painting that this afternoon." Deidre shrugged. "Fiddly work. I need to spend some time with my sister this week finalizing all the furniture and layouts. And I guess I should start planning my wedding, now that we've chosen a date."

Azure laughed. "That last one sounds kind of important. When's the big day?"

"December twenty-eighth." Deidre blew out a breath. "Which is only what, three months away? I don't want anything crazy, but there are still details to work out."

"You'll get married here?"

"That's one of the details, but I think so. I need to make sure my parents are okay with it. They love our church up near D.C., but I don't want all that craziness. They've gone there so long, we'd need to do an open invitation to everyone, and knowing most of those people, they'd come. We'd end up with four hundred people at the thing."

Yet another fabulous reason not to stay in one place for long. Friends were great, there was no question, but staying in a place so long the entire church felt entitled to attend a wedding? Nope. No thank you. "Good luck with that."

Deidre shrugged. "I think they'll understand. They've been down to visit, so I don't have to sell them on the venue, so much as I do it not being a church wedding."

Azure frowned. "Why does that matter?"

"Mom has always had a thing about how weddings are a commitment between two people and God, so they should take place in a church to keep that focus."

"Can't you keep the focus and still set up in that amazing entry hall? I'd think you could. It's not like if you get married outside you're saying you're going to start worshipping trees."

Deidre chuckled. "Exactly. I guess we'll see. The entrance hall though? Really? I was thinking one of the side rooms."

"Like it or not, you're going to need more room than either of the two rooms I saw down here—well unless you used the dining room. If four hundred people would come to the church, surely a group of them will make the trek even if it's down here?"

"I hadn't thought of that." Deidre wrinkled her nose. "Where would you set up in the entrance?"

"Preacher by the door. That way you can make an incredible entrance on that staircase. 'Cause seriously, those stairs were made for grand entrances in dresses with trains." Azure wasn't much for dresses in general, but she'd even be tempted to put one on if it meant she'd get to glamorously sweep down those steps. "With everyone turned to watch? Perfection."

"Hmm. That's something to consider. Thanks." Deidre drained the rest of her water bottle. "You any good with the other details of planning a wedding?"

"Yeah, no. Sorry. I'm just a painter."

"Ha. Artist. Painter does not do justice to your work."

"Speaking of which, I should get back to it. If you need an extra hand with a roller for the rooms upstairs though, let me know. I don't have any particular timeline for needing to be done here. If the murals need to wait so I can help with more basic work, I'm fine with that."

"I'll keep that in mind."

Which meant thanks, but no. Azure had heard it enough times in her life to know that without a second thought. She slipped off the stool, grabbed her thermos, and headed back to the breakfast room. Looked like birds and twining ivy were going to be the sum total of her painting on the job for the foreseeable future.

"Wow."

Azure finished the broad stroke of her brush against the small canvas she'd set up on an easel and turned. The sandy-haired woman standing with her hands in her pockets had an enormous smile and curiosity in her eyes. "Hi."

"That's beautiful." The woman nodded toward the painting.

Azure eyed it and pursed her lips. It wasn't yet, but it was getting there. Still, she was her own worst critic. Most artists were. The appropriate response, then. "Thanks. Can I help you?"

"Oh. No. Sorry. I'm Claire. Deidre's sister? I've been trying to come say hello all day, but every time I'd look up from what I was doing, either Dee would be there with some new urgent thing or you wouldn't be in the breakfast room."

Azure dropped her paintbrush into the jar of mineral spirits, glanced at her hand, and extended it. "Nice to meet you. Did I take too many breaks?"

Claire snorted and took her hand. "No. Please. I saw how much you got done in there and wondered if you were even going to be here a week at that rate."

"The ceiling will be the tricky part. And your sister wants me to touch up some of the other murals—like the peacocks over the fireplace in that tiny little room toward the back of the house?"

Claire rolled her eyes. "That room. What is it for? I think originally it was like a smoking room or something, but it's so small. What are we supposed to do with it?"

"Reading room? Stick a cozy arm chair or something in there. Maybe two if they've got a small footprint. Prayer room? Same general thing. Just a quiet space for one or two people."

"Huh. Quiet room. I like that. I'll try to sell it to Dee. She was thinking of turning it into some kind of glorified coat closet."

Azure winced and shook her head. "That would be a travesty. All that marble? In a cloak room?"

"Exactly." Claire pointed a finger at her and grinned. "So, you paint for a living and for fun?"

"It's all fun. I've never seen the point in doing something you don't enjoy. But I'm actually in a couple of galleries here and there, so this sunset will, most likely, end up hanging in someone's stairwell at some point." Azure cocked her head and studied the canvas. "Or a bathroom. It'd be a nice little pop of color in the right bathroom."

"That doesn't bother you?"

"Why would it? I paint it, the gallery sells it, I get to eat, and someone else has something they enjoy. It's fair all around."

"I thought artists were supposed to be temperamental."

"I can be. Just not usually about my art." Azure shrugged. "Want a sandwich? Since I'm stopped, I might as well eat."

"No, that's fine. I just—" She broke off as her name echoed across the clearing.

A man waved and jogged past the bonfire area toward them. "Claire! Deidre said I'd find you out here. Weren't you coming to church with me? Youth group?"

"Right. I was just getting ready to head back that way." Claire smiled, pink tingeing her cheeks. "Um,

Danny, this is Azure. She's doing the frescoes or whatever they're called."

Danny grinned, his eyes lighting with appreciation as he glanced her way. He extended her hand. "It's a pleasure."

Claire's lips thinned.

Azure hid a wince. The man was obviously clueless. She took his hand for as brief a handshake as she could manage, though he tried to let it linger. "I won't keep you if you're off to church. Claire, it was great to meet you."

"Thanks." Claire's mouth turned down at the edges. "I guess I'll see you around. At least as long as you're here. You really did make great progress today."

Azure hid a smile. Apparently her welcome had just been shortened, at least by one member of the McIntyre family. Well, she had no designs on Danny, and she'd make it a point to let Claire know. Why were men such idiots? "Have fun."

"You want to come? It's always a great time to hang out. And the kids are neat. Most of the Peacock Hill gang is there on Wednesdays." Danny's smile was warm and inviting.

Azure imagined she could hear Claire's teeth grinding together and shook her head. "No, but thanks. Youth groups aren't really my scene."

"Well there's a prayer meeting for adults. You could hit that, but still share the ride down."

"Danny." Claire's voice snapped with impatience. "We're going to be late. She said no."

"What? I'm just being friendly." He cast another smile in Azure's direction.

"Appreciate it, but Claire's right. Bye now." Azure turned. Her mother would be completely aghast at her behavior, but sometimes rude wasn't wrong. Poor Claire. It was clear she had designs on Danny. It was equally clear he had no idea. She'd been there, done that, and had the scar on her heart to prove it.

Deidre poked her head into the breakfast room, a steaming mug of coffee in her hands. "Have plans for the weekend?"

Azure gestured to the blank walls. "Still plenty to do around here."

"Nope. While I appreciate the thought, we're far enough along that we don't really do much on weekends anymore. I realized that I needed to make sure I had a life outside the renovation, and if others are working, I've found I'm compelled to pitch in."

She sighed. Great. "Then I guess not. I'll probably spend some time painting—you have a lovely view out where I'm set up. And there are mountains, so maybe I'll find a place to hike. I guess I'll have to look at the weather."

"Sounds good. You're more than welcome to hang out with us in the evenings, if you like. Fridays are usually pizza and Saturdays generally get decided on Friday. But it's a lot of fun. We play board games or stick in a movie—sometimes both, if we can't all agree. Will you come?"

"Who's we?" Azure set her painting supplies on the table and climbed down from the stepladder, since it seemed like this conversation was going to take longer than a quick hello. And that sounded grumpy even in her head. She forced her lips into a smile.

"Oh. Right." Deidre grinned and sipped from her mug. "Jeremiah—he grabs the pizza, so if you have topping requests let me know and I'll text him. Then Claire and Danny. Although, the two of them aren't a couple, they're just friends, and they'll remind you of that at any opportunity."

She chuckled at Deidre's overly dramatic eye roll. Of course, having seen the two of them on Wednesday, Azure realized it was a clear case of one protesting too much and the other having absolutely zero ability to read the situation.

"Then Duncan and Anna, and Matt usually comes as well. So, see, not all couples."

Right, that's why she rattled them all off as pairs. Well, with the exception of Matt. It was too bad, too, because Matt was easy to look at and fun to talk to, but he'd already relegated her to the *weirdo* category, and experience suggested that was unrecoverable. "I don't know, we'll see."

Deidre opened her mouth then snapped it shut. "Okay. Well, just let me know about the toppings if you decide you're coming. Otherwise, be prepared for nothing that could remotely be considered a vegetable. I've got salad stuff in the fridge though, for anyone who wants to eat like a grownup."

Azure snickered. "Got it. Thanks for the invite."

"One more, before I go."

"Yeah?"

"Sunday morning? Need a ride to church?"

"I usually just spend some time reading the Bible and praying at home on Sunday mornings. Thanks, though." Better to stop there. She was tired of the various reactions her reminder that a person didn't need to go to a physical church building to be a Christian. Look at the people in China who met huddled in basements to avoid detection.

"Oh." Deidre frowned. "Well, the offer stands. Or I can at least give you directions."

"Are there a lot of churches in town?"

"Maybe four? I see what you're saying. Let me put it a different way, we'd love for you to come with us. But it's obviously not required."

"Great, thanks." Azure grabbed her brushes and palette and climbed back up the stepladder. She wasn't trying to be rude. She was here to do a job with the added side benefit of some beautiful scenery to paint. Maybe she ought to figure out where she was heading after here sooner than later, though. If she had a concrete plan, people might be less likely to try and glom on. And if she didn't make attachments, it was easier to leave when the time came.

By three, her shoulders were screaming. Azure climbed down from where she'd been working and arched her back. Maybe that was enough for today. She was making good progress, no one could say otherwise. So, definitely time to call it a day. She gathered her brushes, checked that the paint was sealed, and headed toward the front door. Turning into the entry hall, she nearly collided with a solid mass of man.

"Sorry." Azure instinctively stepped to the side, content to keep going, get her brushes cleaned, and get on with her evening.

"Hey, wait up."

She stopped and turned, finally registering that the man in question was Matt. "Hi. Sorry again."

He grinned. "No problem. I can walk with you if you're in a hurry to get someplace."

He was making so many assumptions, but she couldn't quite work herself up to being annoyed by it. She shrugged. "Sure, I guess. If you don't have anything better to do."

"Afraid not. We finished early at the garage, so we went ahead and closed early. Not many people bring their cars by on Friday night—and if they need to, my cell number's on the front door. I figured I'd come up and see how you were settling in."

"You came to see me?" It was on the tip of her tongue to ask why, but she managed to hold it back.

"Mostly. I mean, I usually end up here on Friday nights anyway, but getting here early meant I might get to see you, and that was definitely a bonus." He tucked his hands in his pockets. "Where were you headed?"

Azure frowned and looked down at the brushes still glistening with paint. "Um. Back to the trailer to clean up."

"Okay." Matt started walking that direction, pausing to hold open the front door for her. "How's it going?"

"Good, I guess? I've got about half of one of the long walls finished. There are some fiddly bits that take longer than I'd like, but that's the way it goes sometimes. Deidre's about the opposite of a hard-driving boss, though."

Matt chuckled. "She's gotten more laid back as things have started finishing up. When she first started it was go-go-go. I think Jeremiah's a good influence on her. He's a big fan of stopping to smell the roses."

Azure sighed.

"What?"

"Smelling the roses is fine, I guess, but I was planning to work this weekend. Deidre basically said that wasn't possible."

"So spend some time hanging out with us, instead. Fridays and Saturdays around here are always fun."

"So I've heard. I already got the spiel about pizza and games or movies." Her legs burned a little as she strode up the hill and around the lake.

"But you're not going to come, are you?"

She paused and turned, hands on her hips. "Why do you care?"

"Maybe I'd like to get to know you."

"You think that's a good idea?"

He frowned. "Why wouldn't it be?"

"You seemed pretty put off on Tuesday by how I've chosen to live. I get that you like my truck, but that's not really a basis for a friendship. Toss in that Deidre, with whom you seem to be good friends, doesn't approve of my church attending habits and I'm not sure why you're bothering."

"What's wrong with your church habits?"

Azure sighed and started striding toward her trailer again. What was it about this guy? His questions should be annoying. As should his persistence, but instead, she found herself bordering on charmed. "I don't think there's anything wrong with them."

"Okay. What are they?"

They arrived at the trailer and Azure pulled open the door. "Come on in."

Matt took a deep breath and followed.

She pointed to the little bench that served as her dining room and desk. "Have a seat while I clean these brushes."

"Church?"

She got down the things she needed from one of the cabinets and began to carefully ensure the bristles of her brushes were free of paint. "I don't go, as a rule. Don't see the point. It's not like sitting in a building somewhere once a week is what makes someone a believer."

"Okay. I can see that. What about fellowship with other Christians though?"

That was one area her life was lacking. Fellowship, in general, was lacking in her chosen lifestyle. "When I find it, it's nice. But it's not a necessity."

"Mentors who can encourage you?"

"I listen to sermons online, read books, even do Bible studies with other people. Church doesn't factor in." She rinsed her brushes under the tap and laid them over the edge of the sink to dry. "What do you get out of it?"

"All those things. Fellowship, teaching, a chance to worship communally. Plus it gives me a place to serve God. I enjoy working with the youth and helping build up the next generation who will, hopefully, continue on serving Jesus."

It sounded good. Reasonable, even. But it all required staying in one place. "I guess it makes sense, if you've chosen to live in the same town for a long period of time. It's not really suited for the way I live."

He nodded. "No plans to change that? Ever?"

Azure reached under the bed and drew out a folding chair. She opened it and sat facing Matt. "This is what I know. It worked for my parents and seems to be doing fine for me. I can go where I want, when I want. What's wrong with that?"

"Nothing, I guess. If you feel like you're doing what God wants you to do, then have at it."

Her eyebrows lifted. That was, perhaps, an overstatement. She was using her talent—one she firmly believed God had given her—but beyond that? It seemed like a tall order to think God cared about whether she drove around from place to place or settled in a neighborhood somewhere. If He wanted her to do something else, wouldn't he make it obvious? "Is that what you're doing?"

Matt ran a hand through his hair as he let out a breath. "I think so. Sometimes I'm not certain, but I haven't had any clear direction otherwise. So for now, I'm working on being content."

"Content is good."

He chuckled. "It is. Now, you've cleaned your brushes, why don't you come down to the house and have some pizza? If you hate it and are having a miserable time, I'll drive you straight back."

He was relentless. And cute. "Yeah, all right."

4

Matt pulled open the door to his truck, his gaze wandering toward the side of the house. Azure had stayed the entire evening, and she'd seemed to have fun, but she was hard to read. Maybe she was even a little bit of a chameleon. She smiled and made all the right responses, but if you caught her at just the right time, it was easy to see her discomfort. It was endearing. And frustrating. He wanted to get to know her—the real her—but it seemed like she kept throwing up shields.

"Hey, Matt. Hold up a sec." Danny jogged down the steps.

"Need a ride?"

Danny shook his head and pointed to his hybrid. "Nah. I was just wondering, um Azure?"

"Yeah?"

"I take it you're looking in that direction?"

Words tangled on Matt's tongue. Azure was fascinating and beautiful. And a puzzle. As a rule, he avoided women like that. Simple, straightforward women who said what they meant and did normal things like living in a house and working a regular job were more his speed. But Azure tugged at something in him like no one ever had. "I guess I am. Yeah. That okay?"

Danny shrugged. "Why wouldn't it be?"

"Well, I have to figure you asked because you were considering it?"

"Maybe. A little. She gave me the brush off on Wednesday, but Claire was out there too, so I think she probably got the wrong idea. I wasn't sure if it was worth trying to straighten things out. I'll let it ride. She's not the only one who thinks there's more going on with me and Claire than there is."

"Why *isn't* there something going on with you two?" Matt leaned his hip against the side of his truck. It was a question that had been nagging at him for close to six months, but he'd never been sure how to bring it up. Since Danny opened the door, though, he had to ask.

"Not you, too." Danny sighed and stared over the top of Matt's truck toward the mountains that were hidden by the dark. "I don't know. She's nice and we get along super well. She's probably my best friend at this point."

"Ouch." Matt clutched his chest.

Danny punched Matt's shoulder. "Quit it. You know what I mean."

Did he? A best friend was a best friend, gender didn't play into it. Or it shouldn't, anyway. So if Claire was Danny's best friend these days, then he and Jeremiah had been replaced. Of course, Jeremiah had Deidre now, and she was edging them out, too. Not that that was a bad thing. It was good. The two of them were clearly a match that God set up. "I guess. So you like spending time with her, she's practically your best friend...why aren't you dating again?"

"There's no spark, man. If I grab her hand, or she brushes up against me? There's nothing. It's like she's just one of the guys."

Matt let out a low whistle. "That's too bad. I'm not sure she got that memo, though."

"Who? Claire? Nah, she's cool. I think she'd say the exact same thing."

Matt wasn't sure about that, but he wasn't going to be the one to try and drum sense into his friend's head. "Well, that works out I guess."

"It does. Except of course that you've got your eye on the only interesting new girl, so I can't exactly put my hat in the ring. It's like Missy James all over again."

Matt laughed. Missy James. He sighed. "She was something else, wasn't she?"

"And still she shot you down."

"Whatever. She wasn't allowed to date. That's not shooting me down, that's being respectful of her parents and their rules."

Danny grinned and shook his head. "You keep telling yourself that, man. The rest of us? We can see a brush off when it's right there in front of our eyes."

"You mean like the one Azure gave you?"

Danny groaned. "All right, all right, you win. If you change your mind, let me know, okay?"

"Sure." To be fair, Matt couldn't guarantee that Azure was any more interested in him that she was in

Danny. She didn't brush him off, but she didn't exactly invite his company, either. Should he mention that? Nah. Better to let his friend think Matt had the upper hand. Maybe if he worked on believing it, it'd become reality.

Of course, his aunt would have something scathing to say about that. She was death on anything that smacked of, what did she call it? Self-help spirituality. So maybe he'd just focus his effort on praying for Azure, and their relationship, such as it was, instead.

"Where's the new girl I'm hearing so much about?"

"Shh." Matt's neck burned as he put his hand on his aunt's arm. "Someone might hear you, Aunt Ida."

"Well of course they might, that's the whole point of speaking, isn't it? I want to meet the new girl they've hired up at Peacock Hill. Azalea or some such." His aunt sniffed. "I don't know what's with people and their bizarre naming trends. But I heard she's doing a real nice job on the painting."

How his aunt heard even half of what reached her ears, Matt had no idea, but it had been going on so long, he'd mostly stopped wondering. "That last part I can attest to. I can take a picture next time I'm up that way, if you'd like to see it firsthand."

"That northern girl, what's her name? The one walking out with your friend Jeremiah? She ought to invite us up. There are a whole bunch of folks who knew that place inside and out who'd like to see what she's done to it."

Matt winced. "I'm sure Deidre plans to do just that, once she gets it finished. You don't want to see it in progress, do you?"

"I don't see what difference that makes, but I suppose the full effect is better." Aunt Ida sighed. "Where'd your uncle get off to now? Go and find him, would you? The organist just climbed up onto her bench and he knows I hate walking in once she's started the prelude."

Matt nodded and hurried out of the church foyer. If he knew his uncle, there'd be a car in the parking lot with its hood open. Uncle Jim couldn't seem to help himself. He could hear an engine that needed fixing from a mile away. Or so it seemed.

He scanned the lot. Sure enough—oh dear. The color and shape of the truck was unmistakable. Hadn't Azure said she didn't do traditional church? That being the case, why were she and her vintage truck in the parking lot?

Matt skipped down the steps and hurried across to where she was parked. "Uncle Jim? Aunt Ida's getting anxious."

Uncle Jim sighed and straightened. "That woman. I love her dearly, but missing the first few bars of the music they play while people get settled isn't going to send me to hell. Still, if I'm not in there soon, I won't have to die to experience a little of it. You see this young lady gets a proper escort into the sanctuary, won't you?"

"Sure." He smiled as his uncle patted his arm and headed toward the building. Turning away from his uncle's retreating form, he offered a smile to Azure. "Fancy meeting you here."

"Claire's car wouldn't start, and Deidre had already left." Azure shrugged and wouldn't meet his gaze. "I was planning on dropping her and turning around, but your uncle really wanted to see the engine."

Matt chuckled and reached up to unhook the bar holding the hood in question open. "It's a family failing. If I offered you lunch after the service, could I talk you into staying?"

"Matt, I—"

"This is purely hypothetical, you realize. I'm just wondering if food works as a lure." What was he doing? He'd flirted more smoothly when he was twelve. A lure? Like some kind of serial killer out trolling for his next victim? He wouldn't blame her if she turned on her vintage sneaker and ran in the opposite direction.

She laughed. "Fine. Hypothetically, the answer might depend on what kind of food is on offer."

This was a dilemma. Did he offer to cook or suggest a restaurant? If he cooked, it was likely his aunt and uncle would try and get them to join their lunch. That wasn't necessarily a bad thing, except, of course, it was his aunt and uncle. Aunt Ida could be an acquired taste. She had a good heart, but sometimes it took people a while to see that.

"There are options."

"Yeah? What kind of options?"

He cleared his throat. "I could grill or we could hit the diner on Main."

Azure pursed her lips. "I happen to be a sucker for well-grilled meat."

"I'll keep that in mind." He knocked on the hood of her truck and glanced over his shoulder at the church. The main doors were shut now, which meant the opening worship music had begun. He wouldn't be sitting up front with his aunt and uncle this morning, apparently. "It was nice to see you."

He turned and started to walk back toward the church.

"Seriously?"

He stopped and glanced over his shoulder. "What?"

"Aren't you asking me to lunch?"

"Oh. Did you want me to?" He bit his cheek to stop the grin that wanted to spread across his face. "In that case, sure. I'd love for you to join me for lunch after the service, if you're interested in sampling my grilling abilities."

"What's the catch?"

"Catch? Well, since I can never guarantee when church is over, it's probably better if you join me for that, too." He cocked his brow. "If that's not too much to ask."

Azure sighed and made a show of locking her truck. "I guess that's fair. Lead on."

Matt grinned. "Come on, then. I promise it'll be worth it."

"I'm going to hold you to that." She glanced up at him and returned his grin before jabbing him in the side with her elbow. "Oops. Sorry."

He bit back a laugh and tugged open the church door. He could add fun to the list of attributes that described the intriguing woman next to him. All in all, she was turning into someone who was going to be very hard to let go when it was time for her to leave.

Matt fiddled with the coals. The grill was nearly ready. He glanced over at Azure, where she lounged on the deck chair with a glass of sweet tea. "So? What'd you think?"

"It wasn't half bad."

He chuckled. "Faint praise, but I guess it'll do."

She shrugged. "I liked the sermon. If your pastor was online, I'd stream him."

"I'll get you the link."

She blinked. "Your tiny church in the middle of nowhere streams their sermons?"

"Sure. Why not? We have people who can't make it sometimes who like to catch up during the week." He reached for the salt and pepper grinders and seasoned the steaks. "And we get a few folks who find us online and listen, then email the pastor. From what I understand, it's become another path to ministry for him."

"Interesting. Technology really shrinks the world, doesn't it?" She didn't sound like she considered that a particularly good thing.

"It does. Nothing beats face-to-face, though." The steaks sizzled as he slapped them on the grill and reached for his own glass of tea. Little beads of condensation dripped down the side. Early September might as well be summer as far as the weather in Virginia. Even here in the mountains, the hot temperatures were hanging on. "You cool enough? I can get a fan if you need."

"This is fine. I have a little A/C unit for the trailer, but I never use it. Or hardly ever. Generally I can get enough of a breeze to be able to sleep. But I also tend to avoid the super hot states in the summer. You make good tea. I'm surprised."

He laughed. "I'm a man of many talents. I learned the fine art of sweet tea mixing as a boy at my Aunt Ida's knee. The key, I'm sure you know, is to add the sugar when the tea's hot. You can get more in that way."

"Super saturation. I'm familiar." Azure took another sip. "Chemistry was one of my favorite subjects in school."

"How'd that work? School?" She'd lived in a bus for crying out loud. Did they just drive the house over and drop the kids off?

"Oh, we were homeschooled. With the way my parents moved around, there was zero point in even pretending we were going to try and use the public system." She shrugged. "It was great. I learned a lot of different skills while indulging my curiosity."

He nodded. There'd been a couple of kids at church when he'd been growing up who'd been homeschooled. It wasn't something he'd ever wished for though. Of course, having Aunt Ida as a teacher—just no. He flipped the steaks. "Almost ready. Let me check the baked potatoes. Need a refill while I'm inside?"

"Sure." She offered him her glass. "You're not going to tell me how weird it is?"

Matt shook his head. "It clearly worked for you."

He took her glass and carried it inside with him. The microwave was beeping. He opened the door and pressed on the potatoes. Soft and burning hot. Probably done. He didn't have sour cream—it wasn't something he cared for, so he hadn't grabbed any. He'd planned to do steak and potatoes for himself and had only bought an extra of each because they made good leftovers. He was a big fan of cooking once and eating for several days off of it. But a lunch with Azure was worth needing to do extra cooking later in the week.

He loaded a cookie sheet with plates, the potatoes, butter, silverware, and their refilled glasses and carried them out onto the deck. "If you want to grab a plate and choose a potato, I'll get the steaks off the grill."

Once the food was served, Matt extended his hand. "Do you want to say grace?"

Azure laughed. "I'll let you do that."

He frowned. "Okay. Do you mind if we hold hands?"

"That's not a line?"

Heat crawled up his neck. "No. Never mind. It's just how we always did it. Um. I can just say my own prayer silently, you go ahead and eat."

"Don't do that. I'm sorry—I—here." She reached across the table and grabbed his hand. "Go."

Matt closed his eyes and tried to gather the thoughts that had scattered at her touch. He took a deep breath and rattled off perhaps the shortest and most inconsequential prayer he'd ever uttered.

Laughter danced in her eyes as she pulled her hand back. "What got you into cars?"

"My uncle. After my parents died, Aunt Ida and Uncle Jim took me in. They were never able to have kids. I'm not sure if they ever wanted to, if I'm honest. But they did it, and I never felt like I was a burden. Uncle Jim ran the garage in town—still does, mostly, though he's working on transitioning it to me—so it was just a natural that I'd go with him. I asked questions. He explained. One thing led to the next, and now he wants to retire and give it all to me." The weight of that legacy was almost palpable. He pushed his shoulders back to try and alleviate the sudden weight on his chest. "How'd you get into painting?"

"Oh. It's just something I've alwa—"

"Hello up there. Matt, honey?"

"Hi, Aunt Ida." Matt's stomach constricted. Ida and Azure was not something he was ready for. He glanced across the little table at Azure and whispered, "I'm so sorry."

"Can I come up? I saw you had company. Jim said it's that girl from up at the hill. I guess he saw the truck at church." Ida's footsteps fell heavily on the deck stairs.

Azure chuckled and slit open her potato.

Matt stood. "Have a seat, Aunt Ida. Can I get you some tea?"

"I wouldn't mind it, thanks." Ida patted his hand and lowered herself into the chair.

"Sure. Um. Aunt Ida, this is Azure Hewitt. Azure, Ida Patterson. I'll be right back." He cast an apologetic look in Azure's direction and hurried into the apartment for another glass of tea. The less time the two of them were alone, the better it'd be for everyone. He loved his aunt, fiercely, but she was an acquired taste—blunt to a fault, she spoke the truth no matter what. It was always done in love, but sometimes a person needed to look close to see that. Most people didn't bother. Aunt Ida's resulting reputation seemed to make her even more determined to be that way.

"...you're set up in some kind of trailer up there. I guess it's better than all those unmarried people living together in one big house, but what kind of woman lives in an RV?"

Azure's smile showed a lot of teeth. "This kind."

Oh great. "Here you go, Aunt Ida. Azure's trailer is actually very homey. I think you'd be surprised."

His aunt turned a narrowed gaze his way. "What were you doing in her home?"

"You've seen her truck." He forced his own smile to relax and slouched into a chair, stretching out his legs in front of him. He glanced at the steak and potato and swallowed. There was no way he was eating with his stomach as knotted as it was now. Guess he'd end up with leftovers after all. "I needed a peek at the engine. Just like Uncle Jim this morning."

Ida shook her head with a put upon sigh. "Typical. You're so fixated on motors, you're missing the fact that there's an attractive, available woman driving it. I'm never going to have grandbabies if you keep that up."

"I didn't miss that." He clamped his lips shut and darted a glance at Azure. She looked like she was trying to hold back a laugh. Maybe it was better than the resigned almost-glare that had been there before, but there was no playing it cool now. He cleared his throat. "And they wouldn't really be grandbabies anyway. I mean, it's not like—"

"Oh hush, boy, before you dig all the way to China." His aunt shot him a disgusted look. "Since we're on the subject of marriage anyway, how long have your parents been married, Azure?"

He blinked. When had they gotten onto that subject? At least it ought to be safe. Azure talked about her family easily, and though their living arrangements were unconventional, the rest sounded solid enough.

"They aren't married." Azure reached for her fork and stabbed a bite of potato.

"Well that's too bad. But divorce happens, even in the church. You're still friendly with both of them?" Ida reached for her tea.

"I am. But you misunderstood. They're not divorced, they've never been married. They'll have been together coming up on thirty years this summer."

"How old are you?" Ida's voice was tinged with suspicion.

Azure chuckle was strained. "I'll be twenty-eight on Tuesday."

"And your siblings?"

"Are all younger. My parents are unconventional and they need Jesus, but they're good people." Azure sighed, pushed her plate toward the middle of the table, and stood. "As much as I wish I could do justice to your nephew's cooking, I find my appetite is gone. I think it's probably time I was, as well. Thanks for trying, Matt."

Panic clawed at Matt's throat and he frowned at his aunt while he stood as well. "Please don't go."

Azure shook her head. "It's time. I'm sure I'll see you around."

"Let me at least walk you out." Matt stepped around his aunt's chair.

"What would be the point? You sit and chat with your aunt. It was nice to meet you, Mrs. Patterson." She lifted a hand in a brief wave and hustled down the steps. The driver's side door of her truck squeaked slightly, and then closed with a solid *thunk* before the engine roared to life.

Matt sagged back into his chair. "Aunt Ida..."

"You're welcome."

"Excuse me?"

"She's entirely unsuitable, and now you know, so you don't have to waste any more time trying to figure it out. *Pfft.* Parents living together like that without marriage? What's the world coming to?" Aunt Ida levered herself out of the chair and patted Matt's arm. "She's pretty, I'll give you that, but you can do better. There's that nice gal down at the grocery in town."

"Who I have no intention of dating. And while sure, her parents aren't doing things God's way by living together like that, did you not miss where Azure said they need Jesus? I'll never understand why you expect people who don't believe in Jesus to live the way He says to. Half the time those of us who *do* believe in Him don't manage it."

"Matthew Patterson! Just because the culture has embraced sin and made it seem like no big deal, I won't have you saying it's okay. I raised you better. Your parents, had they been given the opportunity, would have done the same."

He sighed. "I didn't say it was okay. I said—you know what, never mind. Tell Uncle Jim he doesn't need to come in this week unless he wants to. I don't have anything else to do apparently."

Aunt Ida gave him a long look before shaking her head and moving toward the deck stairs. He heard her mumbling about where she'd gone wrong, but couldn't bring himself to reassure her. He loved his aunt like a mother, she'd been his mother longer than anyone, but she'd also just ruined any chance he might have had with the first woman who'd caught his eye for a good while. Which left him stuck running his uncle's garage in the same small town he'd lived in his whole life, with no possibility of ever getting out. At least a relationship with Azure would've offered something to brighten the inevitable monotony.

5

Azure hopped off the stepladder and rolled her head on her shoulders. She'd finished two of the walls in the breakfast room, and, if she were the one judging, it was coming along nicely.

"Looking good." Deidre grinned from the doorway. "Breaking for lunch?"

"That was the plan. I should be finished in here by the end of next week. The mural around the light in the ceiling is going to be the trickiest part. I was thinking I might try and rig some sort of scaffolding so I didn't have to strain my neck."

Deidre pursed her lips. "I have more ladders and can probably scare up a thick sheet of plywood, if you think that'd work."

That was roughly what she'd been considering. She nodded. "That'd be great, thanks."

"Come on into the kitchen and eat with us."

Us? People were not really on her list of things she wanted to deal with today. Still, it was always smart to remember who was paying the bills. Azure grabbed the insulated lunch bag off the floor and shrugged. "Yeah, okay."

Deidre snickered. "Try to hold back that enthusiasm, would you, you're making a scene."

Azure laughed. Sarcasm delivered that adroitly wasn't what she'd expected from Deidre. She gave off a Disney fairy vibe—all tiny and delicate—it was a constant adjustment to remember that the woman had done the bulk of the restoration here with her two tiny hands. "Sorry. It's a bad habit."

"Happens to the best of us." Deidre pushed open the door to the kitchen. "After you."

Weird, but whatever. Azure stepped into the kitchen.

"Surprise!" The chorus of voices shouted and then broke into the happy birthday song—in about three different keys. Claire was adding cha-cha-cha after each line while Jeremiah and Matt were singing at about Mach 2.

Azure grinned, and then burst into laughter.

Deidre nudged her in the side with an elbow. "We have cake."

"Thanks. How did—" Her gaze zoomed to Matt and she pointed at him. "You."

Matt's cheeks flushed but he held her gaze and nodded. "Guilty. It's not every day someone turns twenty-eight."

Azure shook her head. "Cause that's such an important birthday."

"Hey, every new year is a good thing, right?" Claire winked. "Now, unless you're attached to whatever's in that lunch bag, we have more than cake here."

"I tried to get everyone to wait until Friday so we could have a serious party, but I was out voted." Deidre frowned, her gaze flicking to Matt. "*Someone* was positive we'd never get you to stay Friday night. I thought you had fun last week."

How was it possible for him to read her as well as he did? They hardly knew each other. And yet, even saying that, it didn't feel true. Despite his aunt's interrogation, Sunday lunch was the most enjoyable time she'd had in a really long time. Everything in her ached to spend more time with Matt. It was a seriously bad idea. She'd be finished with work here before September was over. Even if she stayed longer, what possible hope was there for a future for the two of them?

Azure cleared her throat and set aside her lunch bag. "I did. But he's still probably right. This is really nice, thanks. So, what've we got?"

Claire clapped like a little kid. "Yay! I went into town and got subs and some sides from the little grocery store there. It's so much nicer than the big one."

"Sure, but the prices are higher." Deidre shrugged. "It's a tradeoff."

Claire frowned. "It's worth it to support a small business. You of all people should know that."

"I do. It's just—"

Jeremiah put his hand on Deidre's shoulder. "Maybe the two of you could fight about that after the party, when the rest of us don't have to deal with it?"

"Or just let it go and admit I'm right." Claire smirked.

"You're such a typical younger sister." Deidre turned away from her sister and pointed at Azure. "Sit, birthday girl."

"Yes, ma'am." Azure took the seat Deidre indicated and smiled slightly when Matt came around the table to sit beside her.

Matt leaned close to speak quietly. "You're not angry, are you?"

"Why would I be angry? This is the nicest thing someone's done for my birthday in probably ten years. Thank you." Azure met his eyes, hoping he'd see her sincerity. Her gaze flicked briefly down to his mouth—those full lips pulled at her. Heat flooded her face and she looked beyond him to where Claire was loading plates with food. "Are you sure I can't help?"

"We're sure. You sit there and talk to Matt. This was all his idea, so he gets the credit." Claire grinned and handed a plate to Deidre.

Deidre set the plate in front of Azure and whispered, her eyebrows wriggling. "So make sure you thank him appropriately."

Azure swallowed. Was she that obvious? Or maybe they understood that Matt was an attractive man. What woman wouldn't fantasize about kissing him? He was kind and thoughtful too. And a good cook, if his steak and potato on Sunday were any indication. She turned and met Matt's amused gaze. "I was going to grill a steak for dinner tonight. I have enough for two, if you're interested."

One corner of Matt's mouth quirked into a smile, revealing the hint of a dimple. "I'd like that. I promise not to bring my aunt this time."

Azure laughed. "That's a date."

"Is it?"

She pressed her lips together. "I didn't—I mean, only if—it's an expression."

Matt chuckled and leaned closer. "Seems to me, it'll be our third date."

Third. Date. The kissing date. Or so every sitcom on television would have people believe. Unless it was one of those shows where everyone fell in and out of bed with each other simply because they said hi on the street. She didn't usually do a lot of TV watching, it murdered her data rates, but sometimes she'd find a coffee shop with free wifi and spend an afternoon letting her brain rot. Her mother had always said she'd end up regretting it. Looked like she'd been right after all.

Mouth suddenly dry, Azure grabbed the paper cup festooned with balloons that had been placed in front of her and took a long drink. She winced. Whoever made the lemonade needed to become acquainted with sugar. "The first two were kind of disasters."

"You know what they say? Third time's the charm."

She drew in a quick breath, her heart hammering in her chest. Had he winked? His eyelid fluttered—maybe it was just a twitch. She tried to smile as she looked away. She had no business getting involved with someone like him. Not when his family disapproved of her. Not when *he* disapproved of her lifestyle.

So why was she so excited about tonight?

Azure pressed a hand to her stomach. It had been jittery all afternoon. What had she been thinking, inviting Matt to dinner? And why had he agreed? Not that she was upset about that. Still. The list of reasons she shouldn't get involved with Matt were on a repeating loop in her mind.

She dug a couple of red bell peppers out of her mini fridge and rinsed them before slicing them into thin strips and tossing them with olive oil and salt and pepper. It was a lighter nod to including a vegetable, but she didn't figure Matt was going to mind either way. He hadn't even given them a passing thought on Sunday. Unless he counted potatoes as veggies. Technically, she supposed they were, but her parents would have vigorously denied it.

Stepping out of the trailer, she grabbed her tongs and pulled a potato away from the coals. They were ready. She grabbed the other and carried them back into the kitchen where she carefully sliced them in half and scooped out the middles. Twice baked potatoes were one of her favorites, though she didn't usually take the time. But any chance to add extra cheese to something should never be wasted.

"Knock knock?" Matt tapped on the screen door before he pulled it open. "Anything I can help with?"

Her heart took off, beating a rapid tattoo against her chest. "No. I've got it. I just need to put the steaks on. When they're ready, we'll be set. How was the rest of your day?"

Matt shrugged and stepped out of her way as she exited the trailer again with the prepped potatoes and the steaks. "Fine, I guess. We had a couple of oil changes this afternoon. Nothing amazing. I never wish for someone's car to break down, but I miss having more interesting work to do."

Azure chuckled. "Do you guys tow, too?"

He nodded. "Sure, we're in the rotation for who the cops call if there's an issue on the highway. Plus, we get a few locals who need us now and again. We stay busy, it's just not glamorous."

"Glamour is overrated, I'm told." Azure slapped the steaks onto the grate over the flames. "I don't know from personal experience."

"Sure you do. You travel and paint. Your art's in galleries and you're well known enough that Deidre found you to come help here. That's tons better than fixing cars in the same garage you've been working in since you were ten."

"You didn't go away to college?"

Matt shook his head. "Seemed like a waste of time and money. I take classes now and then for new equipment and when dealers change things in their cars. I have certifications, blah blah, but at the end of the day, I'm just a mechanic."

She frowned. "Why do you say it that way? You do important work. The world needs more people who can fix things. Painting is nothing special. Maybe not everyone can do it, I have talent, sure, but at the end of the day, I don't help anyone get from here to there."

"I guess."

"Well, if you don't like being a mechanic, what would you like to do?" Azure flipped the steaks.

"And that's the problem. I have no idea. It isn't that I don't enjoy fixing cars, either. I do. Mostly."

"So it's the location? Why not move? There are mechanics all over the country—the world, even." She pulled the potatoes away from the heat and set them on plates. Touching the steaks she figured another couple of minutes and they'd be ready.

Matt sighed. "Maybe someday. Right now, my aunt and uncle need me. Uncle Jim wants to retire. The garage is mine, if I want it. I've held off agreeing to the formal transfer for close to a year, but I won't be able to do that much longer. He deserves to know if I want it or if he should try to sell. The problem is, I just don't know."

Azure nodded. It seemed the safest response. What would it be like to have expectations placed on her like that? Would it be a comfort or would she, like Matt seemed to, see it more as a burden? She took the steaks off the fire and put them next to the potatoes. She gestured to the table. "Let's eat."

"It smells amazing."

She chuckled and held out her hand. "Thanks. I can say grace."

"I thought you didn't do that."

She shrugged. "The idea's growing on me."

With a slight smile, he put his hand in hers. His skin was rough and scaly. She frowned as she glanced down at it but closed her eyes and tried to steady her thoughts. "Jesus, thank You for this food and for Matt. Thank You for our friendship. Lord, please give Matt guidance about where You'd have him be—if it's the garage here, make that clear so that he'll know he's in Your will. Amen."

He squeezed her fingers before withdrawing his hand. "Thanks. Maybe you could keep praying that."

"Absolutely. What's wrong with your hands?"

"My hands? Oh. Eczema. All the chemicals— from the fluids in the engines to the soap and scrubbing to get them off again—my skin doesn't like it. I haven't found anything that'll completely clear it up. But mostly I don't notice anymore." He shrugged and cut a bite of steak.

Azure considered a moment before digging into her own food. Maybe she could come up with something. Her mother was always fiddling around with various natural remedies for everything under the sun. She'd probably have a suggestion.

"How'd you get into painting?"

"My mother went through a painting stage when I was maybe six. She was never able to translate her ideas onto the canvas the way she wanted to, so she gave up fairly quickly. She thought I had an aptitude though, so they found me lessons. Since I loved it, I was pretty happy about that. And the enjoyment has never wavered."

"Never? Not once?"

Had it? Azure thought back over the years and slowly shook her head. "I don't think so. The closest I've come is the time I took a commission to do a set of portraits for a state politician. Her daughters were not particularly pleasant to work with. But it still wasn't the painting that was the problem, it was the people. I've steered more toward landscapes since then. It's becoming a little of what I'm known for, though I sometimes miss portraiture."

Matt set his fork and knife down and studied her.

"What?"

"Do you have pictures of your work? I've seen what you're doing in the house, but I'd love to see something that's just from your heart."

From her heart. She smiled. He understood better than a lot of people she'd run into. Better than most of her family, if she was honest. They all credited her mind and her talent, but none of those would be worth anything without her heart. "Yeah? After dinner. But remember, you asked."

He laughed. "Did I just sign myself up for the equivalent of my aunt and uncle's slideshow from their trip around the world in the sixties? It's like four hours long, if they do the whole thing."

"Maybe not *quite* that bad."

"Then I can't wait."

Something about the way he said that lifted her spirits into the stratosphere. Had anyone ever been as interested in her as they were in her art? Usually, it seemed, people liked one or the other. She had good friends who cared about her, but didn't really even acknowledge her art—her family was in that camp, too. Or there were the people who focused so singled-mindedly on her art that she might as well not be a living, breathing person without her paintbrush in hand. Matt, on the other hand, seemed genuinely interested in both.

Which made him doubly dangerous.

Azure rolled out of bed and stomped the three feet to the kitchen to press the on button for her coffee maker. She wasn't going to get any more sleep, and tossing around on the mattress wasn't going to help her mood any. And her mood needed all the help it could get right now.

He hadn't kissed her.

She'd let herself get all worked up about it for nothing. And, darn it, she'd been looking forward to it. There was something about that first touch of lips—sure, fine, she still had it to anticipate, but patience wasn't her strong suit. Never had been.

She sighed and watched the dark liquid drip into the carafe below, the siren scent filling the trailer. Breathing in deeply, she closed her eyes. She'd been so sure he was going to, and that made it worse.

They'd spent close to an hour looking at pictures of her art. She'd even pulled out the handful of canvasses she had tucked away under her bed that hadn't made it to a gallery yet. And the work in progress of the view from Peacock Hill. She *never* let people see her works in progress.

Then, when it was getting late, he'd wrapped his arms around her and pulled her close. He'd rested his cheek against her hair and she'd been so sure of what was coming next. But he'd just held her.

That had, in itself, been fabulous. She should focus on that, because as hugs went, Matt had it down. For the time they'd stood there, she'd felt like the only person in his universe. When he backed away—and that had been hard for him to do, she'd seen that in his eyes— she'd been bereft.

But it still wasn't a kiss.

Reliving the hug and questioning what she'd done to change his mind about kissing her had kept her either awake or in that frustrating half-dreaming state for most of the night. Now, the sun was just peeking above the mountains and the golden light of dawn made her fingers itch. Azure dumped the contents of the coffee pot into an oversized mug, found a blank canvas under her bed and dragged her supplies outside.

If she couldn't sleep, she might as well paint.

She set up her easel, took a long drink of coffee, and studied the sky. There was something about the crisp air of an early morning in September that changed the feel of the colors in the clouds. Setting her mug on the ground by her camp stool, she squirted paint onto her palette, dipped in a brush, and let herself go.

"That's beautiful. You did it this morning?"

Azure started at the unfamiliar female voice. She glanced over her shoulder and winced. Her muscles had gotten stiff. What time was it? The woman was pretty. And covered in dirt. "Hi. Thanks. And yeah. I was up early and the light...well, it needed to be painted. Have we met?"

"Not yet. I'm Anna. Hamilton?"

Anna Hamilton. The name was familiar. "Gardener? Engaged to Duncan?"

Anna laughed. "That's me. And you're Azure. Do you get tired of people telling you your name is cool?"

"Never. Cool is better than some of the adjectives I hear. What time is it?"

"Just after seven thirty."

Not late then. That was something. "What brings you out this way?"

"My friend Sean is coming out this morning, probably in about an hour. He's a wedding planner and is trying to convince Deidre that she's ready to start accepting reservations. He's got a bride he thinks would love Peacock Hill. Anyway, he was telling me this woman wants a fun, outdoor reception. I got the idea for a s'mores bar out at the bonfire, so I wanted to see if I was completely out of my mind before I mentioned it to Sean."

S'mores bar. That was clever and fun. Azure grinned. "How big is the wedding? Wouldn't you need to set up tables or a tent or something? I'm not sure the clearing is big enough."

"No idea. It's a consideration, for sure. Although, maybe they could incorporate the lake area and here?" Anna shrugged. "I'll point it out as an option for Sean and let him figure it out. The breakfast room is looking amazing."

"Thanks." Azure glanced back at her sunrise painting. She clearly wasn't going to get more done today. She tried to get down to the house and start by nine. "You want some coffee?"

"Really? I'd love some. I didn't want to wait for it to brew since I had this idea. By the time I get back to the house, I'm sure the pot'll be empty."

Azure gathered her brushes and paint and stood. "Come on. Deidre said you did all the landscaping? From what I've seen, it's great."

"I had help. Duncan—my fiancé—did a lot of it. He got the fountains all working again. Have you seen them running?"

Azure started to shake her head then paused. "The lion head behind the house. I saw that one. There are more?"

"The sunken gardens on either side of the house each have one. Take a look sometime. The rest of the plants need to grow in a little. I think by the end of spring, though, everything will be doing well enough that weddings will be fine." Anna shrugged. "Maybe by then Duncan and I will be married, though we need to get the little cottage fixed up first."

Azure opened the trailer door and gestured for Anna to step in.

"Wow. You live in here? I thought the place Duncan and I were moving into was going to be small."

She chuckled and gestured to the bench while she moved to the kitchen sink and refilled the coffee maker. "Have a seat. And yeah, it's not for everyone, but it suits me. So you'll move away from here when you're married?"

Anna shook her head. "No. If you go all the way down to the driveway instead of cutting across the lawn by the lake, there's a little cottage on the right. Just before the tower?"

Azure had noticed the tower. It speared up into the sky like an ancient battlement of some sort. But she hadn't seen the cabin. She'd pay more attention next time she took the truck out. "Missed it. But that'll be nice, staying here near the gardens."

"Should be. We opened our landscaping business this summer, too. So we're not doing just the grounds here."

"And when's the wedding?" Everyone here was paired off. It was a little disconcerting. Was she drawn to Matt and wishing for his kiss simply because of that? Or were they really as well suited as it seemed? She pressed the button to start the coffee brewing and dragged her guest chair out from under the bed.

"Not sure yet. I've been pushing for something small now. I'm ready for us to start our life together. Duncan's convinced I'll regret it."

"And will you?"

"That's not something I can know for sure, is it?" Anna's voice oozed exasperation. "But no, I don't think so. I don't have any lifelong fantasies about my wedding day. I mean sure, I dreamed about it as a little girl, who didn't? But now I just want it over, so Duncan and I can be together."

"Seems reasonable to me. So why not just choose a date and put as much effort as you can into planning something that's enough wedding for Duncan to be satisfied?"

"That seems sneaky."

Was it? It seemed expedient to her, but Azure wasn't exactly the poster child for relationships. She'd had one serious one and that was before she came to know Jesus. It wasn't exactly something she was proud of now, nor was it something she was going to bring up. "It's not like you have to go behind his back. Just explain you're meeting him in the middle. He wants a more traditional wedding, you're doing that on a small scale and an accelerated timeline."

Anna laughed. "I'll give it a try."

The coffee maker beeped and Azure stood. She took down an extra mug for Anna and filled both with coffee. "I have cream and sugar if you want them?"

"Yes, please."

She stooped to get the small carton from the fridge and grabbed the sugar bowl off the counter. One nice thing about being settled in the same place was the ability to leave things out. If it wasn't in a cabinet or otherwise strapped down when she was moving, it ended up all over the floor. Azure flipped down the small table and carried over the coffee.

"What's next for you, after you finish painting here?" Anna poured a generous amount of cream into her coffee before stirring in two spoonfuls of sugar.

Azure sighed and sipped her own black coffee. "That's the million dollar question. I don't know. Deidre said it was okay with her if I stayed back here to paint. I might do that."

"Is it nice not having responsibilities?"

She frowned. She had responsibilities. Sort of. On the flip side, she did tend to go where the spirit led. Generally, it served her well. She liked it. Didn't she? "I'm not sure I know that, either."

6

"Come on out from under that car a sec, Matt. I need to talk to you in the office." Uncle Jim rapped on the hood of the car.

Matt cranked a bolt tighter and pushed himself out from under the engine. His uncle was already retreating out of the main garage bay toward the office. Matt took the rag out of his back pocket and started wiping at his hands, wincing when he hit the more sensitive skin that nothing seemed to heal completely.

He trudged past the small waiting-slash-reception area that was currently unoccupied. They needed someone to man the desk and phone, but keeping the position filled was more challenging than he'd anticipated. Uncle Jim had tried to explain why hiring high school students wouldn't work out, but Matt hadn't listened. Turned out, all kids seemed interested in doing was getting out of town as soon as they could.

In the office, Uncle Jim sat behind the desk, his hands folded on top of the clear surface. Matt settled into the only other chair—a beat up thing that they'd found by the curb one morning on the way to the shop. It wasn't comfortable, but it held his weight, and that was really all they asked of it.

"What's up?"

"I'm retiring, for good, in December."

One corner of Matt's mouth poked up. Uncle Jim had this conversation with him every six months or so. Aunt Ida was always pushing for them to travel, not seeming to understand that Uncle Jim had no interest in traipsing all over the world unless it was to see some new engine. The man might as well have motor oil in his veins instead of blood. "Yeah? What brought this on?"

"I'm serious this time, Matt. Your aunt's booked us on a month-long cruise. We leave December fourth and won't be back until the New Year. She's already talking about some kind of European bus tour once we recover from that."

Matt's mouth went dry. There were actual plans in place. This was new. And made it a lot more real. "That's only two months. What are you going to do with the garage?"

Uncle Jim opened a thin file and pushed it across the desk. "It's yours, if you want it."

"What?" His voice cracked. This was too much, too fast. "I can't run this place on my own."

"Sure you can. You basically have been for the last four years. And I don't mind popping in when we're in town. You know I'm not going to be happy without my head under a hood. But your aunt's heart is set on this and frankly, I think maybe she's right."

"What do you mean she's right? Right about what?"

"You need the responsibility. It'll help you realize it's time to settle down."

"Settle down." Where was this conversation going? Matt struggled to keep up. How was taking on the full responsibility of the garage going to inspire him to think he had any kind of time for a relationship?

Uncle Jim nodded once. "It's not good for a man to be alone. That's the Bible right there, son, and it doesn't pay to argue with God. You need to find yourself a wife and get busy making some babies. Grandbabies would keep your Aunt Ida at home quicker than anything else I can think of."

"Babies."

"You slow boy? You're repeating everything I say. Come on now, this can't be too much of a surprise. Besides, we thought you having that nice gal with the Studebaker over for lunch might've been the start of something. Was Ida wrong?"

The Studebaker? "Azure? Aunt Ida hated her. She—"

"No, no. The gal seems fine. I'll admit Ida wasn't too keen about the in-law situation, but how often would you see them, anyway? Naw. That girl's the first person you've looked at sideways since high school. In fact, it's Friday afternoon. Why don't you take off, get her some flowers, and drive on over to the city for a fancy dinner?"

He'd had that thought once or twice this afternoon, but he hadn't called or stopped by since

Tuesday. They'd had a good conversation—one of the best so far. Then, at the end, he'd been stupid. She'd clearly expected him to kiss her goodnight. And he'd hugged her instead. He shook his head. "She might have other plans."

"So call and find out." Uncle Jim frowned. "I know I taught you better than this, Matt. Make sure she knows Ida's expecting the two of your for lunch after church on Sunday, too."

"No. Uncle Jim—I can't—I have the Miller's car and I'm only half-way—"

"Pfft. I'll finish that up. You go home, clean up, and go take that girl out. Take this with you, too." Uncle Jim slid the folder across the desk to Matt. "Read it over and sign it and drop it by the house sometime this weekend. Or Monday. Whatever's fine."

"I really—"

"Should get going. Don't worry about the Millers. You're a good boy, Matt, but it's time for you to spread those wings a little."

Dazed, Matt took the folder. He opened his mouth to protest one more time, but the look on his uncle's face had his jaw snapping shut. There was no moving the man once he got that way. He sighed. Looked like he was headed home and then up to Peacock Hill. He'd mostly planned to avoid the usual Friday night gathering on the off chance Azure stopped in.

Could he get away with hanging out at the house without seeking her out? Probably not. His uncle always seemed to know when Matt skirted on the edge of what he'd been told to do.

Flowers. He needed to remember to swing by the grocery store on the way up and get some flowers. Maybe they'd smooth over the awkwardness sure to have been caused by his exit on Wednesday night.

Clutching a bunch of sunflowers, Matt strode around the pond at the back of Peacock Hill, past the little gardener's cottage and the stone tower that speared up into the sky, the top just peeking over the tree line, and headed toward the bonfire circle. Azure's truck was parked. The tightness in his chest eased some. At least she hadn't driven somewhere for her own Friday entertainment. Her small campfire crackled cheerily inside its circle of rocks and music heavy on synthesizers and guitar blared from inside the trailer.

Matt took a deep breath to steady his racing heart and forced himself to loosen his death grip on the flowers. As he lifted a hand to knock on the trailer door, it swung open and smacked him in the head.

"Ow." He clapped his hands to his forehead, the sunflowers bashing into his nose, the little spines on their stems poking into him.

"Oh no. Are you okay? I'm so sorry." Azure grabbed his arm, then let go and stepped back. "What can I do? Do you need ice?"

Matt shook his head and held out the flowers. "These are for you."

"Are you all right?" Azure took the blooms and smiled at them before turning her grin on him. "I'll put these in water. Come on in and tell me what brings you out this way?"

Matt reached for the door at the same time she did, their hands touching on the frame. Little static shocks ran up his arm and he glanced at her. Did she feel it? "I've got it. You go first."

She laughed and stepped in. He watched as she took down a plastic pitcher from one of her cabinets and filled it with water. She set the pitcher aside and unwrapped the sunflowers so she could chop off the bottoms of their stems. "So?"

Matt frowned. "So?"

"What brings you up here? I thought you'd have something to do on Friday night. Or that you'd at least be down at the house eating pizza and watching the marathon of meteor-based end of the world movies that's on the slate."

"That's tonight?" He'd been the one to suggest that theme. Why hadn't anyone told him that was the plan? Not that it would've mattered all that much once Uncle Jim gave his orders, but he might've come prepared to try and cajole her into joining them. He shrugged. "I've seen them before."

"Who hasn't? Doesn't mean it's not a good use of a Friday night."

"So why aren't you down there?"

Azure sighed and fluffed the flowers before pushing them to the back of the counter and leaning against it. "I wasn't sure I'd be welcome if you were there."

"What? Why wouldn't you be?" Of all the things she could've said, that wasn't one he would've predicted. "Of course you are."

"I thought maybe I misunderstood things on Wednesday night."

She wouldn't meet his eyes. Matt rubbed the back of his neck. "It's not that I didn't want to kiss you. I did. I do. I just—it seemed like it was maybe too soon. We've known each other what, two weeks?"

"About that, yeah." She offered a tight smile. "I guess that's fair. I'm not used to guys wanting to wait."

He swallowed. What did that mean? "I don't—"

"I haven't dated a lot since I became a Christian. It's been a tricky thing for me to navigate, frankly. Half the time, I'm not sure if it's really a big deal for people to sleep together if they're in a committed relationship. I mean, sure, the Bible lumps that in with a whole bunch of other sins, but how much of that was cultural and how much is supposed to apply to today? And when I've tried to discuss it, I either get lines and assurances from guys who just want to get into bed, or I get scathing looks from men who'll never speak to me again."

"Okay." He took a deep breath and let it out slowly. He should be used to fielding conversations like this. The kids in youth group seemed to always seek him out when they had questions about sex. But he wasn't. "Wow. Um. So, first off, I promise to keep talking to you. And for the record, I still want to kiss you, too, but that's not really here or there. I guess I don't really think there's any part of the Bible you dismiss as only culturally relevant back then."

"Seriously? There's a ton of stuff that pastors are always saying you have to understand the culture to see the importance of what's being said. And there are all those multiple marriages. If that's not a cultural thing, I don't know what is." Azure turned and opened a cabinet, pulling down a glass. She glanced at Matt. "You want some water?"

"Sure. Thanks." He waited until she handed him the drink, praying that God would give him the right words. "I do agree that it's useful to understand the setting and stuff, but that's not for anything that's a basic right and wrong decision. I mean, if you look at Romans one, none of that has conditions attached to it. God was pretty clear about making man for woman and woman for man in single sets of two. Sure, sin's been perverting that since Satan slithered over to a tree and got Eve to take a bite, but that doesn't change what God wants for us. Sex is how the two become one flesh and I've never understood how anyone can think that can happen with more than one person."

"So, what? If you mess up, that's it?"

Matt shook his head and took a long drink of his water. "No. Of course not. It's no different than any sin, there's grace, it's covered by Jesus. But I do think there are stronger consequences with sexual sin. The way God made our brains, sex is a big deal, and when we make and break those bonds, we can fool ourselves into thinking we don't suffer for it, but it's a lie."

Azure nodded slowly but didn't speak.

Matt finished his water, but it did nothing to soothe the burning that prickled all over his skin. He'd had these types of conversations with teens and with the guys, but never with a woman. He cleared his throat. "I don't know how to segue away from that very smoothly, but I'd planned to ask if you wanted to go get dinner and maybe find something to do after."

She raised her eyebrows.

His face burned. "Not like that. I meant a movie or something."

Azure chuckled. "Gotcha. I'm sorry I made you uncomfortable. But I appreciate your thoughts. And dinner? I think I'd like that."

He brightened. "Really?"

"Really. You wanna drive the truck?"

"Oh, yeah."

She grinned and dug keys out of her pocket, tossing them to him. "Then let's go."

"You should probably put the fire out first?" Matt jerked his head toward the campfire that still burned cheerily outside her trailer.

"Right. Give me a minute. You can go make friends with Jude over there."

He chuckled and ambled toward the truck. A woman he could have hard conversations with and not quite pass out from anxiety and she named her vehicle? There was definitely a lot of potential hiding in Azure Hewitt.

"Where were you last night, man? Hot date?" Jeremiah leaned on the hood and frowned down into the engine beside Matt.

"Date, anyway." Matt straightened with a grin and nodded at Jeremiah's hand. "You're gonna want to move that hand."

Jeremiah put his hands in his pockets and stepped back. "With?"

Matt slammed the hood closed. "Three guesses, first two don't count."

"Heh. Azure. You missed meteor night though. And I don't think we'll be repeating those particular travesties again anytime soon. I'm not sure exactly what you see in those things?"

"They're campy and fun. Maybe I'll see if Azure wants to watch them sometime."

"So you're going to go out again?"

"That's the hope." Matt sighed.

"I sense reservations."

"No. It's not that. She's great and we have these deep conversations, and fun, light ones too."

"But?"

"But my uncle dropped a contract to buy the garage on the desk yesterday afternoon. He's serious this time. Aunt Ida's already got some cruise booked for all of December and she's making plans for a big European tour. I don't know what to do. Am I really going to get stuck here for the rest of my life?"

Jeremiah frowned. "Is that so bad?"

"Isn't it?" Matt paced across the garage and poked at some of the tools on the bench before turning back. "Are you seriously saying you don't want to see what's out there? You're happy here where we have what, two traffic lights and one school for everyone in the county?"

"Maybe not always. But now? Sure."

"Right. Of course. You've got Deidre and Peacock Hill now, so why would you want to leave?" Matt hated the bitterness in his voice, but he couldn't swallow it back. Between Jeremiah, his oldest friend, and Duncan, his newest, there was entirely too much love in the air.

"Sorry, man. Maybe I'm not the one to ask. I do know if you decide to go, I'm gonna miss you. Plus, who wants to drive all the way to Waynesboro for an oil change? If you don't buy, you know your uncle's gonna close the garage."

Jeremiah was right, that's exactly what Uncle Jim would do. It was one more way Matt was backed into a corner. He'd not only be letting down his family—the only family he really remembered—but the whole town. What choice did he have? Matt sighed. "So I'm stuck."

"I didn't say that. I just—where would you go? What would you do?" Jeremiah gestured to the garage. "This is all you've done."

"That's the problem, isn't it? The rest? I don't know. I mean, there're garages everywhere, right? It's not like I want to stop being a mechanic. But here? And then what? Azure's not going to stick around, so that circles back too. What am I doing dating her? If I'm going to be stuck here doing three oil changes a week, it's not like I have anything to offer *any* woman. So then what? I sit around on Friday and Saturday nights while you and Duncan and shoot, even Danny all have families and forget about me?" Matt shrugged. "It's not exactly an enticing picture."

Jeremiah licked his lips and tucked his hands in his pockets. "Have you prayed about it?"

Matt fought the urge to roll his eyes. "Some, yeah, but still no answers. How am I supposed to know what to do?"

"When did your uncle say he needed an answer?"

Had he given a deadline? He'd suggested tomorrow, when he was also supposed to bring Azure for lunch after church. Matt hadn't even managed to get Azure to agree to church in the first place, let alone lunch. "Soon, I guess. He wasn't firm."

"So stall. Look, I was going to hang with Dee tonight, but why don't I put her off and we'll call Danny and the three of us—"

"Four. You'd better go ahead and include Duncan or it'll be weird."

"Good point. The four of us will put our heads together and see what we can come up with."

Matt sighed and picked up a wrench. He balanced it on his fingers, the weight familiar and comforting. Mostly. There was that element of millstone to it as well. What did he have to lose? His friends might have ideas. That was more than he had right now. "You'll make nachos?"

"Of course." Jeremiah grinned as if he sensed victory.

7

Azure crossed her arms and willed the grasshoppers jumping in her stomach to settle as she scanned the crowd milling around the sanctuary. It was just church. Two weeks in a row, though. Did that mean she was becoming traditional? She pushed that thought away. Of course it didn't. It meant she was smitten, that's all.

Matt had oh-so-casually mentioned church on Friday six or seven hundred times. She'd managed to avoid committing, but then he hadn't shown up at the trailer last night. It wasn't like they'd made plans. Still, she'd expected him to simply wander over like he had on Friday and had even made a special trip into town for steaks so she could suggest grilling and hanging out to look at the stars.

He still hadn't kissed her.

She absolutely wasn't going to focus on that right now. She'd dissected that backwards and forwards last night while she ate her expensive beef and moved on to working on her sunrise painting. It was nearly finished. So at least the night hadn't been a complete waste.

She didn't see him anywhere.

"Hey. You came back." Anna grinned and glanced at Duncan, who stood at her side. "Told you."

"You did." Duncan smiled. "It's good to see you again. You want to sit with us? Deidre and Jeremiah will probably slip in late, they always get roped into doing something. I think Matt's with the youth this morning."

Anna nodded. "Pretty sure that's what you told me when you got back last night."

Azure's stomach sank. He wasn't going to be in the service? Why had he invited her? She aimed for casual. "Ah. Well, I don't want to intru—"

"Stop it. You've been up at Peacock Hill how long? You're practically part of the family. Come with us, and I'll make sure we find Matt after the service. Unless you want me to show you to the youth room now? You could hang out down there, I'm sure." Anna's eyebrows lifted.

Azure shook her head. Youth really weren't her thing. *People* weren't her thing, but young people? Nope, nope, nope. "If you're sure."

"Of course we're sure." Duncan chuckled. "I think Sean's going to be coming down again this afternoon, right Anna? You'll get a chance to meet him if you come to lunch."

"I'm not sure what I'm doing for lunch yet. But thanks."

Anna nudged Duncan and mouthed the word Matt.

Azure sighed. So much for being subtle. "So where do you all sit? Maybe we should grab a spot before everything starts."

"Sure." Duncan's eyes crinkled at the corners as he smiled and led the way down the aisle.

Azure cast a longing look over her shoulder at the exit before following. She should've called. Or texted. Something that would have saved her from this.

The service was good, she couldn't deny that. And there was something about being there in the midst of everything that was different than listening to a podcast. Still, Matt's aunt's words echoed in her ears. Her parents were non-traditional. Sinners, certainly, it wasn't as if Azure tried to excuse their lifestyle. Not anymore. But her parents also didn't know Jesus, so why would they live any differently than they did? For all of that, they were honest, which was more than a lot of Christians she'd encountered who lived in very much the same way, but acted like they never did anything wrong.

The pastor, at least, didn't preach as though he was better than everyone. He simply read from God's word and explained how it applied to life—to *everyone's* life, his included. In fact, both weeks she'd come, she'd been amazed at how humble the man was. If Matt's aunt hadn't been quite so outspoken, she probably wouldn't have thought twice about coming again.

Anna's elbow dug into Azure's ribs, dragging her attention out of her thoughts. Everyone was standing for the benediction.

When the song ended and the piano switched to a quiet hymn, Anna touched Azure's arm. "Come on, let's go find Matt."

"Thanks. You can just point me in the right direction, if you want. I can probably find it."

"Nah. The building's small, it won't take long." Anna slipped her arm around Duncan's waist and drew him closer, murmuring in his ear. He glanced at Azure, smiled, and nodded. Anna turned back to Azure. "All right, let's go. They're in the basement."

Basement? Azure hadn't realized the church had another level. "Where do they hide the stairs?"

Anna laughed. "This way."

They wound through little clumps of people chatting, stopping occasionally to say hello when Anna was hailed. Azure was absolutely never going to remember everyone's name, but they were friendly, that was for sure. The stairwell was tucked in the corner of the foyer behind a door Azure had originally assumed was a closet. Stairs led up and down.

"It's bigger than it looks."

Anna grinned. "It is. The property outside is like that, too. Duncan and I are in the process of putting in a prayer garden and making the play area for younger kids nicer. Every time we turn around, it feels like there's a little swatch of land we haven't accounted for."

"But it'll be nice once it's all in."

Anna nodded. "It will. We're working slowly. The budget doesn't have a lot of room for this kind of improvement. So it's going to be at least a year. Maybe two. But we see a little progress as we go and that seems to keep everyone satisfied. Here we are."

Azure stopped beside the door Anna pointed to and peered in the window. A good-sized group of teens milled around inside. Three huddled around Matt, their heads bowed. His mouth was moving but his eyes were closed.

"I'll leave you here. Let Matt know he's more than welcome at lunch at the hill, too, if he wants." Anna patted Azure's arm before heading back in the direction they'd come from.

Now what? Did she go in? Wait out here? She didn't want to interrupt his prayer. But it looked like some kids were leaving through another door. What if he didn't see her?

Pulling her lower lip between her teeth, Azure pushed open the door and slid in along the wall, her gaze fixed on Matt.

"Hey. You're not in the youth group. Can I help you?" A girl with short blonde hair and a mouthful of gum pointed a slender finger at Azure.

"I was hoping to talk to Matt when he's done."

The girl gave her a long, measuring look before nodding. "He's praying with them right now, but you can wait. Might as well pull up a chair though, Mr. Matt's long-winded when he's talking to God."

Azure's lips twitched. "Thanks."

"Sure thing." The girl turned and hollered as she started to jog, "Gina, wait up."

Matt was still praying. He hadn't been one for long prayers the times they'd been together, but then, she'd probably made that unlikely with her commentary. She sighed and settled on the arm of an old, plaid couch that looked like it would eat its occupant alive if they were brave enough to try and sit in the middle.

What was she doing here?

"Thanks, Mr. Matt."

"Yeah, thanks."

"Never a problem, guys. You know where to find me during the week if you need to talk. And you've got my cell. And Jordan, if you're serious about learning about cars, swing by after school, I can always use slave labor."

The gangly redhead rolled his eyes. "I need to earn, man."

"We can talk about that. After you prove you're serious."

"Yeah, all right. Maybe Tuesday?"

"Whatever works for you. I'll be there." The light in Matt's eyes dimmed a little at his words, but his smile was still genuine. What was that about? His gaze moved past the boys and stopped when it reached her. His smile stretched into a grin. "Hey."

Azure lifted her fingers in a half-wave. Why did it seem like there were suddenly so many people around? Her cheeks burned. "Hi. You'd mentioned church on Friday, so..."

"Sorry. The regular teacher for the youth called me last night, late, and asked me to fill in. I should've let you know."

She shrugged. That would've been nice, certainly, but it wasn't as if she'd conclusively said she was coming. "It's okay. I enjoyed the service. I bumped into Anna and Duncan. They invited us to lunch at the big house?"

"Oh. Did you want to do that?" He cleared his throat. "My aunt was hoping we'd join them."

His aunt. "I'm not sure. Um. Does she hate that we've gone out a few times?"

Matt shook his head. "No. She wants to get to know you."

There was no possible way she'd measure up to whatever paragon of womanhood Matt's aunt had in mind for her nephew. On the other hand, Matt didn't seem to mind, and despite any of the objections she'd tried to force into her brain, Azure wanted to spend time with Matt. A lot of it. "Okay."

He grinned. "Do we need to tell Anna and the rest of the gang we won't be there?"

"I don't think so. I told her I wasn't sure what we'd be doing." Or even if the two of them would be doing anything.

"Great." Matt held out his hand, his eyebrows lifting.

Azure hesitated a heartbeat before slipping her hand in his.

His fingers closed around hers, warm and somehow comforting. There was strength there, and it wrapped her completely in a subtle cocoon of belonging.

"Ready?"

She nodded, despite her stomach twisting into knots. "As I'll ever be."

"That wasn't as bad as I thought it would be." Azure glanced down at her hand as Matt linked it with his while they crossed the Pattersons' yard and headed toward Matt's apartment over the garage.

Matt laughed and squeezed her fingers. "I'm really sorry about Aunt Ida. She means well. I know it doesn't seem like it, but she honestly does have a heart of gold."

"I caught a glimpse or two of that today." She managed a slight smile. Matt's aunt had strong opinions and wasn't afraid to use them. Given that Azure often suffered from those same tendencies, she was inclined to give the woman grace, but it was taxing. "I'm still glad I came."

Matt grinned. "Me, too."

So now what? She wasn't ready to head back to Peacock Hill and her trailer. It was a pleasant fall afternoon, she could get plenty of work done on a painting if she put her mind to it, but she just didn't want to. She sighed.

"What's wrong?"

"Nothing."

He stopped and studied her face. "Do you need to go? You said the gallery wanted that sunrise sooner than later."

The gallery. She'd sent them a snapshot of the work-in-progress and they'd replied much sooner than she'd anticipated. They must already have a buyer they think would want it. On the one hand, that was a good thing. On the other, the pressure of that was probably behind her hesitancy to go back and get to it. "I'm okay. I'd rather spend time with you than paint."

"Yeah?"

"Yeah."

Matt gave her arm a tug and pulled her close. He held her gaze as his head dipped. Azure's mouth went dry. Finally. She leaned forward, her heart hammering in her chest as his lips inched closer.

"Matthew Patterson." Aunt Ida's voice had Matt jerking away and looking toward the main house.

Azure closed her eyes as her stomach sank into her shoes.

"Yes, Aunt Ida?" Matt's voice held a hint of resigned annoyance.

"If your young lady wants to stay this evening, Jim thought he'd get out the fire pit and we could roast some marshmallows." Aunt Ida waved and disappeared back into the house.

Matt blew out a breath and shook his head. "She's always had horrible timing."

Azure couldn't fight the smile.

"Wanna go in the garage and see the Stingray Uncle Jim and I are restoring?"

The Stingray. Ugh. Useless car. Sure, it was zippy and had nice lines, but could you even fit a picnic basket in the trunk? Still, in the garage was out of the eye of Aunt Ida and maybe, just maybe, Matt would be inclined to try that kiss one more time. And maybe this time she wouldn't be left wondering what it was going to be like. "Sure."

Still holding her hand, Matt started toward the garage. "She's almost ready. Just a few more hours on the engine and then a paint job and she'll be ready to go. I can't wait to get her out on Skyline Drive with the top down."

"What's special about Skyline Drive?"

"Oh, man." Matt pulled a ring of keys out of his pocket and unlocked the garage door before lifting it to reveal a huge, impeccably organized workspace. The car occupied the middle of the space. It had probably been red. Once. "Skyline goes through the Shenandoah National Forest. Lots of curves and hills. It's a road made for cruising."

Azure nodded and crossed to the car. The interior, at least, gleamed with buff-toned leather shined until it sparkled. She ran a hand across the headrest of the driver's seat. "You did the inside?"

Matt nodded. "Honestly, I've done most of it. Uncle Jim helps by watching and telling me I'm doing it wrong. But I'm counting on him to help with the paint.

That's not my forte. If I had to do it, I'd take it in and let Gage handle it."

"Gage?"

"Works at the garage. He's the main body work guy. He's also at a bigger body shop in Waynesboro, but he likes to work local when he can. If we had the work, I'd keep him full time. As it is, he arranges his schedule whenever I let him know he's needed. That's a lot less often than I'd like." Matt sighed and ran his hand down the hood. "Want to see the engine?"

Azure nodded. "You going red again?"

He chuckled and opened the engine compartment. "It was actually orange. A really gross, not the color it was supposed to be, orange. I'm thinking red, yeah, or maybe green."

"Green would be better." She clamped her lips shut. Why was she offering opinions on a car that wasn't hers?

"You think?"

"Red is obvious."

"Yeah, you're probably right. Blue?"

"Blue would work, too." She leaned in. "You've done a nice job in here, too."

"She's gonna purr."

Azure laughed.

"What?"

"You're such a guy."

"Yes. Yes I am. I thought that might be part of what you liked about me." Matt closed the distance between them and slid his arms around her waist.

Azure's slipped her arms around his neck and leaned closer so their bodies touched. "Might be."

"Well, why don't we see if I can convince you?" Matt's arms tightened around her and his mouth descended to hers.

At. Last. Azure sank into the kiss. Every nerve ending was on fire, but the steady thrum of Matt's heart under her hand kept her grounded. The man could kiss.

Seconds ticked into minutes.

Chest heaving, Matt eased back and ran his thumb over her lips. "Well?"

Azure took a deep breath to try and settle her churning thoughts. She smiled. "I'm almost convinced. Maybe we should try that again, just to be sure?"

Matt grinned, his eyes sparkling. "Maybe we'll plan that for a little later. For now, what would you say to a walk?"

"A walk sounds nice."

Matt took her hand and pulled her close. He dropped a kiss on her forehead before leading her out of the garage. "Let's go then. There's a stream in the woods at the back of the property that I always find relaxing. Maybe you'll decide you want to paint it next."

It'd be a way to stay closer to Matt. A reason to hang out in the area longer. "Maybe I will."

8

Matt hung up the phone and closed the file folder. He pushed it to the front corner of the desk and reached for the next on the little stack of outstanding balances. This was the absolute worst part of the job, but it had to be done. It wasn't like the garage could operate on a charity basis, no matter how much he might prefer that. Uncle Jim had managed to purchase the building, so there was no mortgage, but there were utilities and paychecks that needed to be taken care of, which meant he spent the morning every Tuesday making phone calls to remind folks of their outstanding balances.

"Got a minute?" Uncle Jim sauntered into the room and lowered himself into the guest chair.

Apparently no wasn't an option. He put the phone back in the cradle and closed the folder. "Sure. What's up?"

"I was wondering if you had questions about the transfer paperwork, or if there was something else going on? Why haven't you signed?"

Matt rubbed the back of his neck. "I don't have any questions. At least not that you can help me with."

"What, then?" Uncle Jim leaned forward, resting his elbows on his knees, his hands clasped. "You've always known, I thought, that you could talk to me about anything."

"Yeah, okay. I'm not sure if this is the right thing for me."

His uncle's eyebrows lifted. "I see."

"I don't think you do." How could his uncle understand when Matt wasn't sure he did? "I've lived here all my life. Owning the garage, being completely in charge? I'll never leave."

Uncle Jim nodded. "And you want to."

"Shouldn't I?"

"It's a normal enough feeling, I suppose. Look at your aunt."

Matt smiled. Aunt Ida's itchy feet were legend around town. "I guess I come by it honestly."

Uncle Jim laughed.

"I guess you do. So you don't want the garage?"

Matt's stomach plummeted to the floor. "I didn't say that."

His uncle frowned. "How does that work? You can't run the garage if you're not here, Matt."

"I *know* that." Suddenly, he was back to being a teenager while his uncle explained something simple for the third time because he wasn't convinced Matt understood. "I'm praying about it. I have been since you first mentioned selling. I'm just not hearing an answer."

Nodding, Jim stood, his knees cracking as he did. "I can give you 'til the end of the month. I don't want to push, but I also have to make sure things are settled before your aunt and I leave in December. Be sure you're listening for God to answer your prayers, 'cause He will. He always does."

"Thanks, Uncle Jim." Matt waited until his uncle left the office before lowering his head to the desk. It was a stay of execution, but it didn't solve the problem in the slightest. The end of September was just two weeks away. *God? I could use answers. Clear ones, 'cause I'm apparently not able to hear anything subtle.*

"Knock, knock. You okay?"

Matt looked up at Danny's voice. "Hey, man. I'm fine. What's up?"

"Can you look at my car? It's making a weird sort of sound."

"Okay. Can you be more specific?" Of all his friends, Danny was the least car-minded. It was always amusing to get him to imitate the noises his car made when it was having trouble. More than likely the thing just needed an oil change. Danny was convinced he only had to do that twice a year, despite the fact that he put more miles on it than average with his commute to Charlottesville every day.

Danny shook his head, laughing. "No. I'm on to you. I know you're trying to entertain yourself at my expense. I'm not falling for it again."

"Worth a try." Matt grinned and stepped out into the parking lot. He gestured to Danny's sedate sedan. "Start 'er up."

Danny clicked the key fob to unlock the doors and slid behind the wheel.

Matt shook his head. Danny was also the only person he knew who bothered to lock their car doors in town. He mimed opening the hood and Danny frowned a moment before leaning over. After a long pause, the hood popped up about an inch. Matt unhooked the latch and propped up the cover. Pursing his lips, he listened a moment then walked over to the driver's seat. "I'm not hearing anything abnormal."

Danny revved the engine.

"Ah. Okay." There was definitely some sort of noise. "Go ahead and turn it off. Can you leave it today? You can take my truck."

"You don't mind? I need to get to work—I was hoping I could telework, but there's a meeting I can't get out of."

Matt dug his keys out of his pocket and tossed them to Danny. "I'll give you a call when I have an idea of what we're looking at."

"Just fix it if you can. I trust you."

Matt nodded. That was one definite bonus of small-town living. The people who brought him their cars generally had that same response. He still called. That was his uncle's policy, and it was a good one. The quickest way to lose the trust of the entire town would be for someone to show up and find an enormous bill without warning. "Enjoy your meeting."

Danny rolled his eyes. "Oh, yeah. Sure. At least Julie will be in it, too."

"Julie?"

"I told you about her, didn't I? She's a new paralegal and very easy on the eyes."

Matt shook his head. Was Danny ever going to see the crush Claire had on him? "Asked her out yet?"

"Not yet. Scott moved on her on her first day and she shot him down so fast I think his head's still spinning. I've gotta work out my approach."

"Good luck with that."

"Thanks. I have a feeling I'm going to need it." Danny grinned and hooked his backpack over his shoulder before striding toward Matt's truck.

Matt closed the hood on Danny's car and drove it into an empty bay. At least this would give him something to do besides calling past-due clients. Maybe up to his elbows in an engine he'd get some clarity about his future as well.

Matt slouched in his chair at the back of the youth room. Jeremiah was doing a great job with the devotional. The majority of the kids were listening and the ones ignoring him were, at least, being quiet about it, spending their time on their phones. Normally he'd find it amusing how they tried to hide what they were doing, today it was just irritating. Maybe they ought to bring back the phone box at the start of youth group.

Of course, that had caused a minor riot. Even the parents had been annoyed at the idea of taking phones away from youth for a whole hour. He shook his head. It wasn't as if they wouldn't hear it if the phone rang, so emergencies could be handled. The argument that had finally killed the short-lived idea was that the teens had their Bibles on their phones. Sure, most of them did, but there was a big stack of Bibles at the front of the room. It wasn't as if the kids couldn't use a paper book for youth group and then go back to the app at home. And maybe, if they were actually forced to go old school, they'd be able to look up verses when they couldn't just tap the location.

He sighed. He sounded like his uncle. Did that mean he might as well just stay put and let himself get stuck in the rut that threatened to overwhelm him? Or should he get out, now, while he could still recover from curmudgeonly old man syndrome?

Where would he go? That was the big question. It wasn't as if he wanted to abandon his friends and family. He'd stay close enough that they could still hang out now and then. But what did that translate to? Charlottesville? It was still basically a small town. Not as small as here, obviously, but would it really be any different? So, what? Northern Virginia?

He shuddered. He didn't even like going up there when his friends dragged him because there was some piece of history or culture that he just had to experience. Could he live up there? Maybe he'd talk to Duncan, see if it was more than love that had influenced his decision to chuck it all and start out fresh down here in Hicksville.

"Earth to Matt." Jeremiah jabbed Matt's shoulder.

"What?"

"It's over?" Jeremiah gestured to the clumps of teens laughing and shoveling snacks into their mouths. "What's up with you?"

"Sorry. Just thinking."

"About?"

"The garage. What I'm supposed to be doing with my life. That sort of thing."

Jeremiah nodded. "Any solutions?"

"Not really. Where would I go, Jer? It's not like I want to move to, I don't know, Timbuktu."

Jeremiah laughed. "Richmond? It's bigger, right? But close enough that you can come back for nachos now and then."

Richmond. That was an idea. Why hadn't he considered it? "That's worth investigating. I got stuck thinking about heading up toward D.C. and I don't think I could do that."

"Nope. You'd be miserable. You say you hate small town life, but I don't think you'd enjoy the anonymity of an area like that. Especially not as a mechanic. Places like that? They eat service people alive."

Matt nodded. That was a concern that had niggled at the back of his mind, too. Here, if it took longer to fix a car because a part was backordered, people generally understood. They might not like it, but they didn't give him a hard time about it because they knew him. They knew his family. "You think Richmond would be better?"

"I think you ought to sign your uncle's papers. But if you're determined to go, I think Richmond is a reasonable place to consider."

"I'm not determined."

"Aren't you?" Jeremiah stood. "You say you don't know and that you're praying about it, but I don't see you listening to the answers that I see falling at your feet."

"What do you mean?"

"How much is your uncle charging you for the garage?"

"About fifteen hundred."

Jeremiah nodded. "How many people can buy a fully operational business that isn't in debt for an amount that unreasonably low?"

Matt swallowed. He hadn't looked at it from that perspective before. But still. "That's just because I'm his nephew."

"Is it? If you weren't as good a mechanic as you are? If your uncle wasn't convinced that you'd be able to serve the valley with the same quality of care—or maybe even better—than he'd been providing for so many years, do you think he'd make the same offer? Or would he just close up shop?"

Matt blew out a breath. "He'd close. No question."

Jeremiah nodded and pointed a finger at Matt. "So maybe you ought to consider the fact that you have a deal as sweet as this one on the table to be God's way of answering where He wants you."

Unfortunately, that made sense. "Yeah, maybe."

"Pray about that. Specifically. Maybe you'll get confirmation." Jeremiah stood and gathered his Bible. "And don't be so much of a stranger at Peacock Hill. See if you can't talk Azure into hanging either Friday or Saturday. We'd all like to get to know her better."

Matt smiled. That wasn't going to be easy. She shied away from big group gatherings faster than butter melted in the sunshine. "I'll see what I can do. Thanks, man."

"Anytime." Jeremiah slapped Matt's back. "That's what friends are for."

That would be the one downside of leaving town. He'd miss his friends and his aunt and uncle, although from what it sounded like, they weren't going to be around all that much. If he left, who'd look after their house? What about Azure? The time they'd spent together on Sunday afternoon had been amazing. She'd already captured a piece of his heart. Of course, she wasn't going to stay forever no matter where Matt went. As much as he itched to get out of town, he wasn't someone who could handle a life with no permanent address. So maybe Azure wasn't part of the decision-making process at all. He rubbed his chest to soothe the twinge of pain that thought caused.

He sighed. Was Jeremiah right? Was Uncle Jim's offer God's way of making His will known? He bowed his head and pleaded for the Lord to make it clear.

9

Azure took one last look around the breakfast room and smiled. The birds and twined ivy weren't something she'd rush to have painted in her own house, if she had one, but they suited the space. She'd go find Deidre and let her know the breakfast room was finished. She could start on—and probably finish—the mural touch-ups next week. Which meant what? She could leave by the end of September. Head someplace warmer, maybe.

For the first time in her life, she didn't want to.

It was all Matt's fault. Never mind that she'd practically begged him to kiss her on Sunday. He'd gone ahead and done it, and she hadn't been able to think about much else all week. She'd see him again tonight.

They'd texted back and forth. A lot. And called a couple of times as well. She'd tried to get him to come up and have dinner, but he'd had obligations. She shook her head. He'd even used that word. It was probably good that he was a man who honored his commitments, but she ached to see him. And, instead of a quiet evening alone looking at the stars and, hopefully, sneaking in a few kisses, she'd let him talk her into spending the evening with the gang at Peacock Hill.

Azure poked her head in the kitchen. Deidre wasn't there, but it wasn't empty. A man she didn't recognize was seated at the table steadily plowing through a plate of cookies.

"Hi?"

The man looked up and smiled. "Hi. You must be the painter."

She lifted her eyebrows. "And you are?"

"Sorry." He stood and brushed his hand on his jeans before offering it. "I'm Sean Fitzgerald."

Sean. That was familiar. She came the rest of the way into the kitchen and shook his hand. "Oh. Event planner, right?"

"That'd be me." Sean resumed his seat and pushed the plate closer to the center of the table. "Cookie?"

"You know what? Why not?" Azure pulled out a chair opposite Sean and selected a cookie. "What brings you out here?"

"Came down for the weekend. I'm working with Deidre on her wedding plans. Two months are going to go by faster than she realizes. Plus I have another client I really want to get booked for April. Deidre keeps insisting they won't be ready, but Claire says they will, and when it comes to organization, I trust her a little more than her sister."

Azure grinned. "Known them long?"

He shook his head. "Not really. I've been friends with Anna for years though."

"Right. I guess Duncan's given her the inside scoop."

Sean chuckled. "And she passed it along. I peeked in when I got here, the breakfast room's looking great."

"Thanks." She flushed with pleasure at the compliment. "Finished it up this afternoon. I was looking for Deidre to tell her. I figure I can touch up her murals next week and be done, unless she has something else she needs me to do."

"What's next?"

Azure shrugged. "Not sure yet. I might hang around for a bit. There's plenty to paint up here."

"Anna took me out by the bonfire when I was up last—you're living in that trailer?"

She nodded.

"Starting to get cold at night, isn't it?"

"A little. Usually around this time of year I start heading south, but I've got some good quilts, I'll be okay for a while longer." Granted, if it dipped into the forties overnight too many times in a row, she might be rethinking the offer to stay in the house. Or maybe that'd be her signal that it was time to move on. For now, she was managing with blankets and thick socks. "So, April. Isn't your bride getting anxious about not having a venue?"

Red colored Sean's cheeks and he cleared his throat. "She *might* think it's already locked in."

Azure laughed. "You have a backup plan, I assume?"

He shook his head. "They want an outdoor wedding. Even if there's something in the house that isn't perfect, the outside should be fine. And the s'mores bar was genius."

"Yeah. She's going for that?"

"That's the plan. Of course, Deidre heard about it and might be trying it out first."

"At the end of December?" Southern Virginia might not be a winter wonderland of snow, but surely it still got too cold for outdoor receptions.

"I'm working on an idea to do it indoors. I've seen table-top s'mores before. Worst case scenario, we'll use the fireplace in the dining room."

"That works?"

Sean nodded. "Deidre assured me it did. Granted, not too many people can cook a marshmallow around it, but then, they're not having a big affair."

"There's still going to be cake, right?"

He laughed. "Absolutely. I haven't met a bride yet who didn't want a cake."

Azure had. Her sister had donuts instead. Granted, they were stacked on top of one another as if to make a cake, but they hadn't cut through them to make slices. Nope. Everyone had gotten a donut on a plate. It was odd. But then, that suited Indigo down to her toes. Still, she and Windfeather seemed happy enough the last time Azure had spoken to them. They'd settled in a little artist commune in Arizona and, from what they said, earned enough from tourists to provide everything they needed.

Everything except Jesus.

None of her siblings or her parents understood Azure's conversion. Was she doing enough to try and reach them? Her family was scattered to the four winds and not big on communication.

She reached for another cookie.

The kitchen door swung open and Azure glanced over her shoulder. Deidre strode in, a frown etched into her features.

"Hey. You okay?" Sean stood and gestured to the plate that still held quite a few cookies. "We have cookies."

"A cookie isn't going to fix a leaking shower." Deidre growled low in her throat. "But it might keep me from wanting to kill someone, so sure."

"Would it help to know I finished the breakfast room?" Azure scooted her chair over a smidge to make room for Deidre to sit beside her. "And I think the murals will be quick."

"It doesn't hurt." Deidre bit into a cookie. "Oh yeah. These are Claire's work. That girl should be cooking somewhere, not sitting here organizing me."

"I don't think she'd be here if she didn't like what she was doing." Sean brushed the crumbs on the table in front of him into a neat pile.

"I guess. She doesn't seem happy, though." Deidre lifted a shoulder. "Just one more problem for another day. You made good time from Richmond, I'm glad you could join us. Duncan's looking forward to having company on the third floor."

Sean laughed. "I didn't realize we were having a slumber party."

Deidre's frown finally completely eased. "Yeah, I can't promise that." She turned to Azure. "You're staying tonight, right?"

Azure nodded slowly. She'd been trying to figure a way out of it all afternoon, but Matt was determined. "Matt said it's game night?"

"That's the plan. Claire suggested Fictionary."

"What's that?" Azure contemplated the plate of cookies. She'd already had two. That was probably enough.

"Basically, someone gives a word from the dictionary that they think is hard and that no one will know. Everyone makes up a definition and writes it down. Then, when everyone's done, the person who gave the word in the first place reads all the definitions and people say which one they think is right. Whoever gets the most votes, wins a point." Deidre smiled. "It's fun. There's actually a version you can buy, where the words are on cards, but those words are too easy and half the fun is digging through the dictionary to find something weird. Although, Anna's a bit of a word nerd since she worked in the library, so she sometimes guesses the actual definition."

That didn't actually sound terrible. Azure nodded. "I think I'm going to head back to the trailer and clean up before supper. That okay?"

"Of course. Come back whenever, but by five thirty for sure." Deidre reached for a cookie. "And bring your appetite. Claire said she was making stuffed shells."

"Yum. Nice to meet you, Sean."

"Same. See you later." Sean stood as Azure hopped down from her chair.

Azure gave a little wave and headed back out through the dining room to the entry hall that never ceased to put a little catch in her breath. She turned and stood, gazing up at the stained-glass depiction of peacocks that graced the first staircase landing. It was impressive. And beautiful.

If someone had to put down roots, might as well do it in a grand style like this.

"I still don't think that's a real word." Matt frowned and reached for a cupcake off the platter in the center of the long table that had been set up in the dining room.

Azure shook her head. "It was in the dictionary."

"Yeah, but who put it there?" Matt pointed his finger. "I still think it was one of y'all."

Everyone laughed and began clearing the table.

Azure studied Matt.

"What?"

"I never would've pegged you as a sore loser. It's fascinating."

"Sore loser? I'm not a sore loser. I just don't approve of cheating." Matt crossed his arms.

Jeremiah laughed and leaned across the table. "Don't let him kid you, Azure. He's been a bad loser his whole life. Except in football."

"Yeah, well, in football, you get to smash the heck out of people. If they beat you after that, they won fair and square." Matt crumpled the cupcake wrapper into a ball and tossed it back onto the platter with the lone remaining treat.

"Seriously? Football? Ugh." Azure made a gagging motion.

"What? No way. It's—that's—you're un-American." Matt stared at her. "You're kidding, right?"

"Homeschooled, remember? It's not like I had a school team to cheer for. And the professionals? What's to love about a bunch of grown men in tight pants running around on a field for enough money to feed a small African nation for a year?" Azure paused and pursed her lips. "The tight pants are okay."

Deidre laughed and slid into the seat next to Jeremiah. "Yes, yes they are. That's basically the only reason to watch the game."

"Philistines. Both of you." Matt frowned at Jeremiah. "Did you know about this considerable lack in your future bride?"

"Sadly, yes. But I love her anyway." Jeremiah slung an arm around Deidre's shoulders. "Are we really having s'mores at our wedding reception?"

Deidre nodded. "That was Anna's idea, by the way. So don't blame me."

"Whoa. I never—" Anna held her hands up in front of her chest.

Jeremiah laughed. "I'm good with it. It's just different. But different can be good."

Sean cleared his throat. "Speaking of the wedding, do you two want to go over a few things now?"

"That's my cue to leave." Claire grabbed the last of the dishes off the table and headed into the kitchen.

Danny nodded and tucked his hands in his pockets. "I'll see if I can help Claire. You can't possibly need my opinions on anything wedding related."

"You mind if we hang and listen?" Anna nudged Duncan with her elbow. "We should start thinking about wedding stuff. Like dates, that sort of thing."

Duncan had half-risen from his chair. He frowned and sank back into the seat. "Right. Of course we should. I was just thinking that."

Matt shook his head. "Sure you were."

"Thanks for inviting me to play tonight. It was fun." Surprisingly. Even the obviously paired-off-ness of everyone there wasn't too horrible. Of course, Matt hanging on her every word hadn't hurt. In fact, maybe they were part of that whole coupledom thing. That was an interesting thought. Her heart stuttered in her chest. Was he thinking they were headed toward marriage like all his friends? Her mouth went dry. That was not in the plans. She scooted back her chair and stood. "Goodnight."

Matt stood so quickly his chair clattered to the ground. "Can I walk you home?"

Jeremiah snickered and Deidre jabbed him in the side with her elbow.

"Sure. I'd like that." Azure rubbed her hands on her jeans, suddenly unsure what to do with her arms. She strode from the room before she could say or do anything that would embarrass her further. Although, she probably didn't need to be embarrassed. She liked Matt. He liked her. But, did everyone think it was something more serious than it was?

"Hey, wait up." Matt jogged to her side as she arrived at the front door. He reached for her hand. "Everything okay?"

"Yeah. Sorry." Azure curved her fingers in his.

He pushed open the door. "Did you have fun?"

"I did." Azure paused on the front steps and breathed in the crisp fall air. "Gosh, it's a pretty night."

"It is. But then, most nights in the fall are like this up here." He gave her hand a little tug and led her down the stairs and toward the side of the house. "Have you toured the gardens yet?"

"Not really."

"Let's take the long way back then. Is that okay?"

More time with Matt? "Absolutely."

He grinned, his teeth gleaming in the moonlight. They rounded the side of the house and descended three steps into a sunken garden area. A fountain burbled cheerily in the center of the pavers that made up a patio. The plantings around the border were just visible in the low light.

"I bet this is nice and cool in the daytime."

Matt nodded. "Duncan spent a lot of effort this spring getting the fountains to work. I think they're on timers now and shut off around nine. I guess maybe we should've done this when it was lighter."

Azure chuckled. "It's nice. I can still get a feel for it. Show me the rest."

"You're sure?"

"Yeah. If nothing else, it's time alone with you."

Matt turned and pulled her to his side. "Thanks for spending time with my friends tonight."

"I enjoyed it." Azure pressed a kiss to his cheek. "I like this, too."

"So do I." Matt led her up a set of steps to a large, grassy area bordered by knee-high hedges on either side. A pergola stretched across the far end. "These, I'm told are going to be enclosed gardens. One is open in the middle, for smaller, more private weddings. The other has a windy path with more private nooks for pictures or assignations."

"Assignations? You really were reading the dictionary tonight."

He chuckled. "It caught my eye, I'll admit. Come on, you need to see Lover's Lake."

She laughed. "They aren't really calling it that, are they?"

"I don't think so. Not officially, at least, but it's what everyone seems to say."

They walked hand in hand across the grass and through the pergola. They wound along a path, under the shadow of the stone tower that speared into the night sky, and finally reached a lake surrounded by trees.

"I walk past this—or at least near here—every day. But I haven't really paid attention to how beautiful it is." Azure stopped, her gaze roaming over the idyllic spot. She turned to face Matt and slid her arms around his waist. "I think I understand the nickname."

He smiled and held her close. "I'm starting to get a glimmer myself. Azure?"

"Yeah?"

"I told my uncle I'd buy his garage today. He's wanted to retire for a long time. As much as I want to travel and see the world, I believe God's calling me to stay here. Bloom where I'm planted, if you will. I still plan to travel—there are slow periods when I could close and take those trips—but...I thought you should know."

Azure pulled her gaze away from his and looked over his shoulder at the trees swaying in the light breeze. She'd known he was settled. Everything about him oozed a desire for hearth and home. She should never have started down the path to a relationship with him. She'd known that, too. "Congratulations."

"Hey." He touched her chin, gently swinging it around so their eyes met again. "You'll be here a while longer, won't you?"

"I don't know, Matt. I'll be finished with my work next week. Maybe...maybe the smarter thing to do is head south now. Before things get more complicated than they already are." She blinked against the moisture that pooled in her eyes.

His whole body sagged and he stepped back, away from their embrace. "Let's get you home before it gets too late."

A tear slipped down her cheek. Azure swallowed the burning lump in her throat and nodded. It already was.

10

The door buzzer sounded and Matt pushed himself out from under the car he was currently working on. He grabbed a clean rag off the workbench as he passed by on his way into the reception area. "Deidre? What brings you here?"

"I was hoping you could do the safety inspection on my car, actually. I just realized it was due in September."

"And today's October second."

Pink flared across her cheeks. "Yeah. Sorry."

"It's fine. As it happens, there's no line today." Matt jerked his head toward the garage bays. "Why don't you bring 'er around for me?"

"Also?"

He stopped mid-stride and returned his gaze to hers.

"I found this on the table in the breakfast room. It has your name on it. I'm fairly certain Azure would've preferred to give it to you in person though, if you hadn't made yourself scarce all last week."

He cleared his throat and reached for the small jar. There was piece of paper folded and taped to the lid with his name scrawled across it. His heart ached. It wasn't like staying away had been easy, but it had been the right thing to do. Azure made that clear. "It seemed like it was best."

Deidre shook her head. "Best for whom?"

"Everyone. Look, it's complicated."

She snickered. "People say that all the time when what they really mean is they don't want to talk about it."

He shrugged.

"Fine. If you don't want to talk to me, don't. But anyone with eyes could see she was hurting because you weren't around. It seemed like things were going well—what happened?"

So much for not having to talk to her about it. Matt sighed and set the jar down on the reception desk. "I bought the garage from my uncle."

Deidre grinned. "Congratulations. That's great news. How is it possibly a problem?"

"Because it means I'm rooted here indefinitely. Permanently, most likely. And Azure lives in a trailer that she drives wherever the wind blows. Do you even know where she's headed?"

"Atlanta."

Matt's eyebrows lifted. He hadn't expected there to be a plan.

"She said she had a gallery excited about the landscapes she'd painted while she was here, so she was going to drop them off."

"Ah. And then?"

Deidre frowned.

"Exactly. She doesn't know. Wherever she ends up. How does someone who lives like that settle in downtown Hicksville with a mechanic?"

"Settle? So it was serious."

Matt looked away, studying the curling edges of the oil filter advertisements that lined the wall beside the ancient soda machine. "It was getting there."

"Do you love her?"

Love. The word stuck in his throat like a bite of overcooked chicken. And yet, wasn't that exactly what he'd thought he was heading toward? Still, better to hedge. "I was headed in that direction. I wouldn't say I was there yet."

Deidre nodded. "So why'd you give up?"

"Didn't you hear anything I just said? What's the point? I'm here. She's everywhere else. If I thought there was a chance for even three seconds, I would've asked her to stay, but as soon as I told her about the garage, she was mentally packing her bags." Matt snorted. "Gimme your keys and I'll get that inspection taken care of."

"Matt." Deidre clamped her mouth shut when he shot her a look. Shoulders falling, she dug keys out of her pocket and tossed them to him. "Okay. Thanks."

He nodded and pointed to the machine. "Sodas are free, if you want one."

He pulled Deidre's car into the garage bay, honking the horn and flicking on the wipers as he did so. The sticker was expired, so that was something. At least

Deidre had been telling the truth about that. It was just convenient that it meant she could come harass him about Azure.

He rubbed his chest. Would the ache ever ease? A week without seeing Azure and it hurt more than it did driving home from Peacock Hill after game night.

Working quickly, he checked the brakes and fluids and double-checked that Deidre wasn't also due for an emissions inspection. Everything looked great. He scraped off the old sticker and replaced it with a new one with next year's date on it before backing the car out and parking in front of the main door.

"You're all set. It's fifteen."

Deidre stood, setting her soda can aside as she crossed to the register. "I can't help but think you're making a mistake with Azure."

"That's because right now you're looking at life through love goggles."

"Love goggles?" Deidre snickered. "What are love goggles?"

"You're engaged, so you think there's a happily ever after for everyone else, too. But the reality is, what you and Jeremiah have is unique and rare. I'm glad the two of you found each other, I really am, but you can't expect the same results all the time." He ran Deidre's card and handed it back. "I appreciate the thought, but let it go, okay? I'm good. Or I will be."

Her shoulders slumped but she nodded. "All right. You're sure?"

"Sure." He could fake it, at least, until he figured out exactly how to make being okay a reality. It wasn't even just the situation with Azure. It was the whole deal with the garage and his aunt and uncle, too. The future was suddenly stretching out in front of him, and he didn't know what to do with it.

"How'd it go today without me?" Matt's uncle settled onto the sofa in the apartment above their garage and propped his feet on the crate that served as an extra chair or a coffee table as needed.

"I think I'm going to hire a receptionist. Someone who can manage the paperwork and cash people out, answer the phone, all that kind of stuff. There's no way I can keep up with all that when I'm going to be the primary person working on the cars." Matt brought his uncle a glass of iced tea and sat next to him. "Why didn't you ever have someone?"

"Your aunt Ida did it for a while. Then we realized she'd do better getting a job with more earning potential so we could save for retirement. I guess maybe it was before you started helping out. It's definitely easier with someone there. If you can find the right person. You know the margins we run at. Finding another full-time salary in there isn't easy."

Matt sighed. That was true. But the fact remained, he couldn't do everything himself. He'd burn out before his aunt and uncle even left for their first vacation. There had to be a solution. He'd add it to the enormous list of things he was praying about. "Are we working on the car tonight or what?"

Uncle Jim chuckled. "Let me see your hands."

Matt frowned and held them out. "Why?"

"Your skin was so cracked the other day, I didn't want to push you to use your spare time if you'd be better off giving them a rest. They still don't look great."

"Yeah. Nothing seems to work." He stood and crossed to the kitchen counter, grabbing the glass jar Deidre had dropped off that afternoon. He brought it over to the couch. "Just got something new to try. Maybe it'll help."

"Looks homemade. Azure make it for you?" His uncle gave him a sly look. "Haven't seen her around lately. Been busy up at the hill?"

Matt winced. Of course his uncle noticed. Or, more likely, Aunt Ida did and sent him over to find out what was going on. "She's gone. But yes, this is from her. Deidre dropped it off for me."

"Gone? What do you mean, gone?" Uncle Jim reached for the jar and frowned at the note. "You read this yet?"

He shook his head.

His uncle tugged it off and handed it over before unscrewing the jar. He held it up to his nose and sniffed. Pursing his lips, he dipped a finger into the thick cream.

He gave it another sniff before rubbing it into the back of his hand. "Smells kind of like a juniper tree, but I imagine there's more in it than that. Feels nice going on."

Matt clutched the note in his hand. He'd assumed it was simply a label. Now, he could see there was more writing and he wasn't sure if he wanted to read it. What could she possibly have to say? Then again, maybe it was a list of ingredients.

"Try some." Uncle Jim thrust the jar at Matt and stood. "Tomorrow we'll work on the Stingray. Maybe with you handling all the work at the garage, I'll tinker a bit during the day, if that's okay."

"Yeah. Sure. You're not leaving?"

His uncle nodded. "Might as well get back before your aunt comes looking for me. I don't know what happened with you and that young lady, but you're a good boy, Matt. A man any woman would be proud to call her own. You'll figure it out."

Matt managed a weak smile. "Thanks."

When his uncle had gone, Matt stared at the note a moment before setting it aside and, instead, sniffing the jar. There were hints of something pine-y. Leave it to his uncle to know the exact tree, though. It wasn't unpleasant smelling. Or feminine. Aunt Ida had purchased more creams and lotions than he could count, but there was no way he was walking around a garage smelling like roses and baby powder. He tapped the surface of the cream and brought the glob of lotion to his nose. Definitely not feminine. With a shrug, he rubbed it into the most cracked area on his left hand.

It tingled ever so slightly. Not a bad sensation, as if he'd put something caustic on an open sore, but like how muscle creams tingled when they were rubbed in. He scooped a little more and massaged it into both hands. It couldn't hurt. If it helped, well, all the better.

He screwed the lid back on and eyed the note. Was he really this much of a coward? Just read the thing. It was probably a list of ingredients, or a website where he could order more of the cream. Given the glass jar and printed label, the stuff was clearly from some small business. If it worked, he'd be happy to get more. Azure had probably wanted to make sure he could do that without needing to contact her.

Heart sinking at that though, Matt steeled himself and grabbed the note. He unfolded it and his breath caught. Her handwriting was lovely. The scrawl of his name on the front would never have suggested there'd be flowing script inside. But then, she was an artist, and that fact was made obvious in every aspect of her life.

Dear Matt,

My mother makes a lot of different lotions and creams from shea butter and essential oils. I asked her what she thought might help with your hands, and this is what she sent. I'm not sure if it's a recipe she already made or one she concocted just for you, but either way, if it works and you run out, she'll be able to make you more. I'll put her contact info at the bottom of the note.

I'm not completely sure why you disappeared this week, although I have an idea. I wish you hadn't felt it necessary. I would have liked to spend more time together, even though I guess there really was no point. You're rooted here, and that's not a bad thing.

It's like what Paul says in Ephesians, that we're to be rooted and grounded in love, and while I know he wasn't talking about the love of family and friends, that's every bit as much a part of your root system as the love of Jesus.

In some small ways, I envy you.

My family isn't big on roots. We talked about that. I'm not convinced I'd even know how to grow them if I were to try. I certainly have no examples of how it's to be done. In spite of that—knowing nothing between us could ever work long term—I care for you. Your withdrawal hurt. But then, I suspect—even, perhaps, hope a little—my leaving hurt you.

You have my cell number. Text me some time, would you?
All the best,
Azure

She'd included her mother's email and website underneath her signature. He sighed and set the note on the crate, pinning it in place with the jar of hand cream. She cared. What did that mean? People cared for all sorts of other people without it being romantic, that's what friendship was, wasn't it? A sort of caring?

Had he misread the entire situation? His face burned. Those kisses. He didn't go around kissing women he *cared* about.

Blowing out a breath, he grabbed his phone and opened a text message.

"Got the jar and your note. Thanks. Sorry I didn't say goodbye." There was so much more he could add, but why? She couldn't possibly care. He laughed. There was that word again, *care*. Before he could talk himself out of it, he hit send.

Now what? There was never anything worthwhile on the television. He could go see what Jeremiah or Danny were up to, but they were likely to ask probing questions about where he'd been all last week. He wasn't sure he had the answers. Or, if he did, that they were worth sharing. Maybe he'd go down and work on the 'Vette. If Uncle Jim could work solo while Matt was at the garage, seemed reasonable that he could put in a few hours on his own, too.

As he stood, his phone buzzed with an incoming text. Something fluttered in his chest. Had she written back that quickly? He sat back down and swiped the screen.

"Me, too. I should've hunted you down. I meant what I said in the note."

Matt rubbed the back of his neck. She cared. Just not enough to try and figure things out. Of course, he'd gone and hidden, which wasn't really the best way to convince someone there was anything to figure out in the first place. So, he was definitely also at fault. He tapped at the screen.

"I care too. I wish there were a way to make this work." His finger hovered over the send button. Was it too much? Too straightforward? He punched send. If it was, so be it. Better to get it all out in the open than keep skirting around the edges. Would she reply?

Seconds ticked into minutes.

His phone buzzed. This time with an incoming call. The picture he'd taken of Azure filled his screen. He answered.

"Are you serious?" Azure's voice was full of insecurity.

"Yeah. I was serious when you were here, too. But you didn't see your face when I told you about the garage. I also know when I'm playing a losing game."

She sighed, her breath crackling in his ear. "I'm sorry. I was surprised. Maybe I shouldn't have been. You'd mentioned the possibility. You'd also mentioned wanting to travel."

"Trust me. I know how confusing it is."

She chuckled. "I guess you do. Why'd you agree to your uncle's terms?"

Matt settled back against the sofa cushions and propped his feet on the crate. How could he explain something he wasn't completely sure of himself? "Ultimately, it came down to doing what I felt like God was telling me to do. All the doors that led away from here were closing—sometimes violently—but this one was open."

"I guess I can see that. But what about seeing the world?"

"I'll work it in." He would. Finding someone to handle the paperwork and cashing out was a big step in that direction. Uncle Jim had never wanted to hire help—not at a wage that would keep them in town. Maybe it wasn't feasible, but Matt was going to try. "For most people that's called vacation, right?"

"I don't know. My family isn't most people."

He frowned. "And you've only ever paid attention to your family?"

"All right, fair point. Yes, I guess that's how most people make it work. It doesn't feel, I don't know, restrictive?"

"Of course it does. Why do you think I fought it? But it's not like God promises us a footloose and fancy free life. He put us here on Earth to work. So that's what I'll do." She was quiet. Had he upset her? He ran back over the words and winced. Maybe it had come across as criticism of her choices. "Which isn't to say there's anything wrong with moving from place to place. I guess it boils down to listening to where God wants you."

"Yeah. It's hard to tell sometimes."

"Tell me about it." He reached for his iced tea and took a long sip. "So, where are you?"

"Oh. Right. Atlanta for now. There's a gallery here that does a lot for me. The owner was excited about the sunrise I did at Peacock Hill. I have enough sketches to do another one or two paintings and make it a series. So, I'm set up at a campground a little outside the city, and I'll work on those. He's already said he wants them when they're ready."

"And then?" The weather was getting colder. It was unlikely she'd be headed back up this way, but he couldn't stop himself from asking—from hoping.

"I don't know. My folks usually end up in either Florida or Arizona for the winter. I often join them for a couple of weeks. It's a chance to catch up. Sometimes my siblings make it around the same time. But I'm not sure."

"Okay. Well, would you mind if I texted or called occasionally?"

"I'd like that. Matt—I'd love for us to find a way to make this work."

Everything in him warmed. It was a fantasy, of course. How could it work when he was here and she wasn't? Still. "I'd like that, too."

"Okay. Well. I'll talk to you later?"

He grinned. "Yeah, of course. Good night."

"Night."

Matt ended the call and scrubbed his hands over his face. He believed God was a God of miracles. And that was what it was going to take for him and Azure to have a chance at love.

11

Azure stepped back from the canvas and arched her back. She'd been painting long hours all week, taking only occasional breaks when Matt texted or her stomach complained loudly enough that she had no choice but to put something in it. On the positive side, this painting was nearly finished.

She had another painting in mind already. She'd snapped a few photos on her cell phone that captured the general idea, but she wanted to expand on it. Of course, since it included the house, Azure was tempted to offer it as a thank you gift to Deidre. Maybe she could use it somewhere in her decorating efforts. On the other hand, it wasn't like Azure couldn't make another painting of the place, and with the gallery asking for any of the paintings she made on the theme, maybe it was better to sell the first and find out if Deidre would even be interested in having one. For all Azure knew, Deidre didn't want to put anything on the walls.

As she reached for her water bottle, her phone rang.

"Hi, Mom, what's up?"

"Hi yourself. Can't I just call my daughter?"

Azure laughed. "You can, but you don't."

"True. You know me too well."

"So? What couldn't wait for an email?"

"Your father and I bought a house."

Azure blinked and sank down into the chair by her little camp table. "I'm sorry. I thought I heard you say you'd bought a house."

"Funny girl. That's exactly what I said, and you know it. Dad thinks he's found a buyer for the minibus, too."

Azure's mouth opened, but she couldn't make words form. "I—"

Her mother chuckled. "That's basically the same response all your siblings have had. To answer the questions that you'll think of later, it's in Arizona, near Flagstaff, so reasonably close to Indigo and Wingfeather. Just two bedrooms, but then, it's still more space than we're used to. There's a little yard, but not a lot, and it isn't as if there's a lot of maintenance required."

"It sounds lovely. But why?"

Mom sighed. "Because you can't travel forever. Dad and I found we were spending more and more time parked in one spot, loathe to move on. Neither of us wanted to be the one to suggest settling down, but when we finally talked about it, we realized we were on the same page. You know we've always loved Arizona, so it made sense. Will you come for Christmas?"

Azure struggled to wrap her mind around the picture of her parents in a house that didn't have wheels attached to it. "Christmas?"

"Yes. You know, December twenty-fifth? Presents? Santa? Ringing any bells?"

"Yeah, I just—I'm still working on you and Dad in a house. Sorry. I hadn't figured out where I wanted to be for Christmas yet." A picture of a snow-covered mountain rising behind a modest home and it's above-the-garage apartment came clearly to mind. A crackling fire. A tall tree, decked out in red and green and white. Hot chocolate. And Matt. Was that even possible? Her mother was still talking. "Sorry, go back. I missed that."

"I'm interrupting your work, aren't I? I'm sorry. Call me later."

Azure glanced over at the nearly finished painting. "No. This is fine. I got distracted. Can I let you know about Christmas later?"

"Of course. We're not going anywhere."

Azure snorted. "No, I guess you aren't, are you? Send me your address."

"Oh, speaking of that. If you want to drop your P.O. Box and have your mail sent here, we're happy to collect it and send it out as needed. It'd save you a couple of dollars a year."

"Yeah. Um. I'll think about that, too. I don't think I'm renewing until January." Thoughts swirled in Azure's head, but she couldn't grab hold of any of them long enough to do anything with it.

"How's fall in the mountains? And did the hand cream help?"

Azure's heart sank. Hadn't she texted her mom about leaving? Her questions made her think of Matt all over again. She'd just managed to push him out of her mind. She tried for breezy. "I'm in Atlanta, actually."

"Oh. Well, that's always fun. And the lotion?"

"Matt said he thinks it might be? He's only had it a couple of days." She swallowed and wished, again, that she was there to see the results for herself.

"Hmm."

"What?"

"Why'd you leave?"

"My work was done, the gallery here was anxious for the paintings I'd mentioned. It was time." Azure could hear the defensiveness in her voice, but was helpless to do anything about it. "I'm okay, Mom."

"Oh, honey. If you have to say it that way, I know you aren't."

"Maybe not. But I will be." She swallowed the lump in her throat. She would. She had to be.

"Do you want me to come to you? I'll get on a plane if you need me."

"No, Mom, I really am okay. Promise."

"If that changes, let me know. I'm serious. I love you, Az."

"Love you, too, Mom. Bye."

Azure ended the call and blinked back tears. Longing for Matt was a quiet, constant ache in her heart that never seemed to ease. If her parents could settle and put down roots, could she?

"You're an artist, huh?" The short, stocky man leaned against Azure's truck and snapped his gum. "What brings you to our little campground?"

Azure sighed and set down her paintbrush. When she'd checked in, there'd been a comfortable, matronly woman manning the desk. She'd pictured the woman's husband as a grandfatherly teddy bear sort, not this. He oozed enough smarm to make her skin crawl. Trying to appear unobtrusive, she reached for her phone. "I work with a gallery in Atlanta. Dropped off a few pieces earlier this week, but they were excited about some proposals I made, so I thought I'd work on them here while I was in the area."

"Nice. You ever take breaks?"

"Not really." Maybe if she didn't ask return questions he'd get the hint and keep moving. Her fingers curled around her phone and she prayed that God would protect her.

The man stepped closer. "How much did the wife charge you for the week? I can get you a break, if you want to make a trade?"

Azure took a step back, her hands balling into fists. "I'm fine, thanks."

"You sure? I hate to see a lady alone and unprotected."

Yeah, right. He probably looked for them wherever he went. Before she could answer, her phone rang. Azure answered quickly without looking to see who it was. "Thanks so much for calling when you said you would."

"Azure? You okay?" Matt's voice was a mix of confusion and concern.

"Probably. You remember where the campground is, right?" She rattled off the address and prayed Matt was smart enough to catch on.

"Am I calling 9-1-1? I can do that for you."

"Hold on." Azure hadn't taken her gaze off the man, but she cupped her hand over the speaker of her phone. "Can you excuse me? This is an important call."

The man grunted and gave her a long look, lust in his eyes, before shuffling off.

Azure sagged against her trailer.

"Hey. Talk to me. Do you need the police?"

"Matt. I'm okay. He left."

"What do you mean? What's going on?"

"Just a guy hassling me. He's one of the campground owners. I hadn't realized the place was as empty as it is. When I checked in there were a handful of families staying." Her heart was gradually slowing to its normal speed. "It's good you called when you did. I was trying to figure out what to do."

Anger vibrated through Matt's words. "Find somewhere else to stay. I mean it."

She stiffened. Who was he to lecture her? "I don't think it's going to be a problem. It's the weekend. I'm sure more people will be coming."

"Don't be an idiot! If there's a creepy guy threatening you, you move. This is common sense one oh one."

"Idiot? Really?" Azure took a deep breath and blew it out. It didn't help at all. She took another and ground her teeth together. "For your information, I've been on my own since I was eighteen years old. I know how to take care of myself."

"Do you? Cause it doesn't seem like it. What were you going to do, throw your phone at him? Splash him with paint?"

Since those were two of the ideas that had flitted through her mind, Azure clamped her mouth shut. She'd also considered screaming, although that was unlikely to have done anything beyond make the man laugh, seeing as there was no one else around.

"Do you at least have your phone set up so you can contact emergency services without having to look at what you're doing?" Matt's voice had calmed, but there was still an undercurrent of tension.

"Of course." Didn't she? Wasn't that standard? She just had to turn it on and then tap the bottom of the screen where it said *emergency*. Even if not, she wasn't going to tell Matt. She'd figure it out when the phone call was over. "But I think you're overreacting."

"Am I? Then why did you answer the phone and give me your address like you needed help? How often does something like this happen?"

"Not often." There were creepy people everywhere. It was a fact of life. She'd learned that early on and, generally, was able to spot trouble and avoid it before it became an issue. She'd obviously missed something when she checked in here, but that didn't mean she was completely incapable of taking care of herself.

Matt's sigh crackled in her ear. "I don't like you being off on your own like this where I can't help you if you need it."

She bristled. "I don't need your help."

"So you've said. You don't want it either, obviously. I'll let you go. Please find somewhere safe to stay. If you won't do it for yourself, do it for the people who care about you?"

The flat silence on the phone made it clear he'd hung up. Azure closed her eyes. She'd paid through next week. She was unlikely to get a refund, even if she managed to catch the woman in the front office instead of the man. Her paintings sold okay, she didn't hurt for money, but losing a hundred and fifty bucks was still a lot to swallow simply because Matt was worried about her. Plus, she'd have to find somewhere else to go and that was going to cost money, too.

On the other hand, as much as she'd assured Matt more people would be checking in today for the weekend, she wasn't nearly as positive as she'd sounded. It was the first week of October. Even though temperatures were still mild in Georgia, the number of people camping was considerably lower than in the spring and summer.

She glanced over at the painting. She'd finish it and drive in to the gallery to drop it off. And then? Azure eyed the front of the campground. The man was sitting out in front of the office smoking a cigarette, his chair angled so he could keep an eye on her.

She swallowed but couldn't get the taste of metal out of her throat.

Maybe losing the money wasn't such a bad idea after all.

"You really are welcome to stay in the house. You've been with the gallery so long it feels like you're family." Crystal Branson stood out of the way while Azure unhooked the trailer from her truck.

"I appreciate that, I really do, but I'm fine out here. Are you sure you won't get in trouble with your neighborhood association? I didn't see any other RVs."

"I'm sure. You'll be here what, another week? Two? If anyone asks, I'll mention that we have company. I'll also try to keep the kids out of your hair, but when the boys get home from school, they're going to want to look at your truck. They've been after Rob to let them go in together on a car and fix it up to drive." Crystal shook her head. "As if Rob has any idea about cars."

Azure laughed. Rob was the artist behind the gallery's success. Crystal handled the business end of things. It seemed to work well for their marriage. Their two boys were a freshman and a junior in high school and crazy about girls and cars from what Azure had pieced together in conversations with the Bransons. "What about you? Do you know about cars?"

"Oh, no. I'd still get full service gas if it was an option. The less I have to do with a car, the happier I am."

"Well, send 'em out. I'm happy to give them some basics. I really do appreciate you letting me park in your yard." Azure crossed her arms and forced herself not to think about the near altercation with the man at the campsite when he'd seen her hooking up her trailer. Matt had been right to insist she move, but she probably would've come to that on her own.

"If it gets Rob the last two paintings in what he's calling your 'Blue Ridge Series,' I'm all for it." Crystal grinned. "You sure you won't at least come to dinner?"

"I don't want to impose."

"It's no imposition—it's spaghetti. Come at five thirty, okay?"

After a day like she'd had, she'd been planning to spread peanut butter of a piece of bread and call it a day. Spaghetti she didn't have to cook sounded like a dream come true. "All right, twist my arm."

Crystal chuckled. "I'll leave you to get settled, then. Come on in the back door whenever you want."

Azure opened the trailer door and climbed inside. She'd tossed her furniture in rather than stowing it properly. Thankfully, nothing had shifted too much. Before long, the little table and chair were set up on next to her on the driveway. With an hour before Crystal expected her for supper, Azure wasn't sure what to do. She stretched out on her bed. After a moment, she curled into a ball and shook as the near horrors of the day washed over her.

12

"What's eating you?" Jeremiah tossed a soda at Matt before turning back to the jalapeños he was chopping.

"Why do you think something's eating me? What does that even mean? It's a stupid phrase." Matt popped the tab on the soda can and took a long drink. Maybe he should've bailed on the guys' night at Jeremiah's, but after a long Saturday at the garage, he was ready to unwind with friends. If they were going to let him unwind instead of asking stupid questions.

"Uh huh. That right there is what I'm talking about. You're grumpy, and that's not usually you." Jeremiah scooped up the peppers and dropped them into a little bowl. He walked to the sink and scrubbed his hands before turning, leaning on the counter, and crossing his arms. "Spill it."

Matt sighed. "Azure."

"Ha. I knew it. Go on." Jeremiah grinned.

Matt shook his head before relating the incident at the campground yesterday. "So, it's good that I called when I felt that little nudge to get in touch, but she hasn't returned any of my texts checking in on her. She's apparently stubborn enough to stay someplace she isn't safe simply because someone with more sense than she has suggests she ought to move."

Jeremiah cleared his throat. "You do know women don't like being told they're incapable of taking care of themselves, right?"

"Even when it's true?"

"From what I've gathered? Especially when it's true. She was scared and you yelled at her. That's not really going to win you points."

"I don't really care about points if her life is in danger. I'd rather she was alive and ticked off at me than any of the other possible alternatives out there."

"So alive and in love with you isn't something you'd like better?"

Matt rolled his eyes. "You know what I mean."

"I do. Just checking."

Matt sniffed as the scent of chips, ground beef, and cheese began to waft from the oven. "Don't let those burn."

"Pfft. Please. Who's the nacho king?"

In spite of everything, Matt laughed. "Nacho king? Nice. So, if you're so smart about women all of the sudden, what should I have done?"

"Expressed concern calmly and then asked what she thought she was going to do to ensure the situation couldn't happen again."

Matt snorted.

Jeremiah shook his head.

"Oh. You were serious? That's what you would've done if you called Deidre just before some creeper could rape her?" Matt tucked his hands in his pockets and made his voice high and prissy. "I would like to express my concern calmly..."

"Okay, okay." Jeremiah laughed. "You seriously should never make that voice again. It's terrifying. Did you at least apologize?"

"She won't return my texts. I thought that was something I should do in person."

"Normally, I'd agree with you, but if she's being stubborn, you should at least text the apology."

"Can I say I'm going to call the cops if I don't get some kind of response because I'm worried?"

Jeremiah winced. "I might hold off on that a little longer."

Matt huffed out a breath and grabbed his cell phone. "Fine. When are Danny and Duncan getting here?"

"Should be any second."

Matt tapped out a short apology and hit send. It took every bit of self-control he could muster not to add the bit about the police, but Jeremiah was probably right. No need to antagonize her again. Yet. Even if he was concerned that she was lying broken and bleeding in her trailer. Or a ditch.

"Knock, knock." Danny and Duncan shouted in unison. After a couple of seconds they clomped into the room.

"Nachos again?" Duncan wrinkled his nose.

"Why do we invite him again?" Matt shook his head at Duncan. "He has no class."

"He's my future brother-in-law, I don't figure I can get out of it." Jeremiah frowned. "But we do need to work on his taste."

Danny laughed. "It's so nice not to be the butt of everyone's jokes anymore. I'm glad you're here, Dunc."

"Yeah, yeah. I suppose after our manly meal of chips, meat, and cheese we're going to do other manly things like run around shooting aliens?" Duncan poked at the sodas in the ice bucket and finally grabbed one.

"I was thinking you could all teach us macramé instead tonight. That work for you?" Jeremiah opened the oven and pulled out a sheet tray loaded with steaming nachos.

Matt laughed and pulled a plate off the top of the stack before bumping fists with Jeremiah. "Nice one."

Danny grinned and got himself a plate.

"You guys are nuts, you realize that?" Duncan got in line behind Matt and Danny. "Just for that, maybe I'll leave the turtle brownies Anna made us in the car."

"Wait. You brought brownies?" Matt turned to eye Duncan. "Go get them."

"I'm not convinced you deserve them." Duncan shrugged and casually looked over the nacho toppings.

"Dude. Go get the brownies or Matt and I will spend the evening trying to see if we remember how to give a swirlie. We were pretty good at it at one point in high school."

Matt laughed at Danny. "Do you remember—what was his name? Jordan?"

Danny grinned. "Oh, yeah. That was epic."

"The two of you would get expelled and charged with assault if you were kids today." Duncan frowned and pointed his finger at them. "I'll go get the brownies, but then you have to look at wedding invitations with me and help me choose my top three in order."

"Wait. What? No way." Danny held up his hands. "I am not part of the Peacock Hill wedding mania."

Matt shrugged. Normally, he would've been right there with Danny, but now? He got a glimmer of a picture of Azure in a flowing white dress walking toward him. Maybe wedding details weren't so terrible after all. If she ever spoke to him again.

Seemed like that might be a big if.

Matt grabbed his toolbox and hopped down from his truck. He glanced up at Peacock Hill and couldn't stop his smile. The old house gleamed now. It was a far cry from a year ago when Deidre had come to start fixing it up. He climbed the stairs and banged on the front door.

"Hey. Thanks for coming." Sean extended his hand to Matt with a grimace. "If you need to tow it, so be it, but if you can fix it here, that'd be better. I brought my spring bride down and she's not going to be pleased if we can't make it back to Richmond this afternoon."

Matt chuckled. "I'll do what I can. You're the silver SUV?"

"That's me. Here are the keys. It made such a weird sound when I cut the engine, I tried turning it back on and got nothing. Figured I'd better call someone right away rather than waiting until we were done with our appointment here." Sean sighed. "Any chance of talking to the painter lady? The bride has it in her head that she wants a portrait painted of the two of them. That's not something I've tackled before."

"Unfortunately, Azure's on her way to Arizona right now." It was a tiny miracle he knew that much. Her texts, once she finally acknowledged him again, had been brief and impersonal. Any calls he tried went straight to voice mail. Sure, Matt knew she'd been busy with the last paintings for the gallery—and he was glad they'd offered her space at their home to do it—but he missed her voice and the easy conversations they'd had. He'd apologized as many times and ways as he knew how, but she stayed distant. "I can mention it next time I talk to her if you want."

"Would you? Give her my number and I can get her details. Maybe she can work from a photo and wouldn't have to head all the way back here?"

Matt shrugged, deflated. The possibility that a commission would bring her back here where they could talk in person had glistened like the pot of gold at the end of a rainbow. For exactly four seconds. Sean was likely right—she could work from a photo and stay in Arizona. Or wherever. "I'll mention the idea. Do you have a card or something so I can give her your details?"

Sean reached into his shirt pocket and extracted a card from a small stack.

"Thanks." Matt tucked the card into the back pocket of his jeans and gave a little salute. "I'll come find you when I know something about your car. Will you be inside?"

"Probably? Maybe give me a call and I'll let you know."

"Sure." Hefting the toolbox again, Matt took the stairs two at a time and crossed the driveway toward Sean's car, gravel crunching under his shoes. He clicked the fob to unlock the doors and set his tools on the ground by the hood before climbing behind the wheel and starting the engine.

No lights on the dash lit up. Nothing sounded off. He pulled the lever for the hood and slid out of the car. Might as well give it a look before declaring this a colossal waste of time. It didn't take long, everything seemed to be in order. With a sigh, Matt closed the hood and shut off the engine. No strange sounds then, either.

Maybe Sean needed his hearing checked.

He pulled the business card back out of his pocket and frowned at it. Might as well text it to Azure now, before he had a chance to lose it. He snapped a picture and added a quick note about Sean's bride to the text. Then he punched in the number while he headed back toward the house.

"That was fast."

"It seems fine."

Sean laughed. "Of course it does. Sorry, man. We're in the kitchen if you don't mind coming in?"

"That's fine. Be there in a minute." Matt ended the call and shook his head. He put his tools in the back of his truck before heading into the house. Someone had been polishing the wood—the scent of lemon hung in the air, warming it. The parquet floors gleamed.

Deidre popped out of the front room. "Oh, hi."

"Hey. Sorry, guess I should've knocked. Just bringing Sean his keys back. His car's fine."

Deidre fell into step beside him. "Wasted trip, sorry."

"All in a day's. Anyway, I got to see you, so that's something."

Deidre chuckled. "Should I warn Jeremiah that you're going to object at our wedding and try to get me to run away with you?"

"Do I have a shot?"

She swatted his arm. "No."

"Then no." He grinned, some of the tightness in his body loosening. He needed to remember that he had friends here. Azure being gone didn't mean his life was over. Or even really different.

"You all right?" Deidre paused with her hand on the kitchen door and held his gaze.

"I don't know. Women are mystifying. I'll get over it." He shrugged. "We doing games or a movie on Friday?"

"Movie, I think. Jeremiah wanted something with a lot of explosions." Deidre made a face.

"Whatever. You love them as much as the rest of us."

"My secret's out." She grinned and pushed open the kitchen door. "Hey, Sean."

"Hey. You met Larissa, right?" He glanced at the woman seated next to him. "Larissa, this is Matt, sorry I don't know your last name."

"Patterson." Matt held out a hand then frowned and waved instead. "I run the auto garage in town and I'm all dirty. Sorry. Nice to meet you. I'm biased, 'cause I've always loved Peacock Hill, but I don't think you could've chosen a better spot for your wedding."

"Thanks. I just wish Tom—that's my fiancé—could have made the trip, too. I'm making all the decisions and he's not here." Her lips twisted into a wan smile and she shifted her gaze to Deidre. "Sean says you're getting married soon, too? Is your fiancé like that?"

Sean flashed a meaningful look at Deidre.

"Um. A little, sure?" Deidre cleared her throat. "I just came in for a bottle of water. It was good to see everyone."

Matt put Sean's keys on the table. "I think you're set. If for some reason you end up having trouble when you're finished, give me another call."

Following Deidre from the kitchen, he touched her arm. "Jeremiah's up to his eyeballs in wedding plans."

"I *know*. But did you see Sean's look? That poor girl's clearly on edge. I was trying to be reassuring."

Matt shook his head. What was more reassuring than the truth? Wasn't it better to know she should go home and kick some sense into the man who wanted to spend his life with her? Whatever. Not his problem. "Any chance you know where Duncan is?"

"Yeah, they're out at the cottage cleaning. Why?"

"Thought I'd poke my head in and say hi. Maybe see about getting something a little more presentable than the one scraggly bush we have in the median planting at the garage." Matt shrugged. The front of the garage looked worn down. Uncle Jim had never seen the point in doing much about it. He'd said the proof was in the work they did. But people today shopped with their eyes, and since Matt had ideas about a website, which would need a photo of the building, there was some sprucing up that needed to get done.

"Want me to call and check?"

"Nah. I'll walk out. Gage has things in hand at the garage for right now. Stretching my legs would be good."

"Okay. Hey—next time you talk to Azure, tell her we miss her."

Matt snorted. "You'd be better off doing that yourself. Trust me."

13

Azure watched as her mom and dad pulled fake spider webs out of their plastic packages and strung them on the shrubs and rocks in their front yard. "Don't you think you're taking it a bit far?"

"Honey, it's Halloween. Did you see what all the neighbors have done? We don't want to stand out as unsocial. We have all that candy we need to give out tonight." Her mom grinned and put her hands on her hips. "I think we need some around the door."

Dad grinned and tossed another bag at her mom. "You do it. You've got the better eye."

"I still don't think—"

Her dad cut her off. "Let it go, Az. I'm sure you have some superior reason that Christians don't participate in the holiday, but keep it to yourself, okay? Your mother and I try to respect your choice to be religious, even though it's not how we raised you. The least you could do is loosen up enough to let kids have candy."

Azure snapped her mouth shut and turned on her heel. She'd been with her parents a little over two weeks and it was time to move on. Past time. When they'd settled down and bought a house, she'd hoped they might move a little more mainstream in some of their other thoughts, too. If anything, they were determined to be the weirdoes on the block. Oh sure, they were loveable weirdoes, but adding one adjective didn't change the other.

Just like every time she'd wanted to leave since she arrived in Arizona, the next question was: where should she go? Her heart pulled her back to the mountains. Not just any mountains, though. The Blue Ridge called to her. *Matt* called to her.

Azure rubbed her chest over her heart. Things between the two of them were almost back to where they'd been when she left Peacock Hill. They could be completely fine if she'd let them. She was holding herself back. She knew it, but she couldn't seem to stop. He'd been so over the top about the incident in Atlanta. And right. He'd been right, too. Which one bothered her the most?

She sighed and opened her trailer. She'd finished the portrait of the bride and groom for Sean. Maybe she should start heading back that way and see what happened. Deidre had been texting her off and on and had sent an invitation for Thanksgiving. And for her wedding. What was it about that group that made her feel like she was part of them when she'd only been there a few weeks? It wasn't just Matt. But he was certainly a large part of it.

If she got on the road by lunch, she'd have a good four or five hours of driving before she needed to stop. Azure got her phone and opened up her map app, following the main Interstate east, she frowned. Could she make it to Albuquerque today? She double-checked the distance and nodded. That was doable.

Flipping over to her browser, she hunted down a couple of campgrounds and made a note. She also found a cheap motel, in case the campgrounds didn't pan out. She wasn't staying anywhere she was the only guest again. That was a promise she'd made herself.

Azure looked around the inside of her trailer. She was mostly ready to go. It took only a few minutes to stow the items she had out. She took a deep breath. What would her parents say? Only one way to find out.

She hopped down, locked the trailer door, and headed in through the side door of her parents' house.

"Mom? Dad?"

"In the den, honey." Her mom sounded cheerful as always. Nothing much ruffled her feathers. Her dad, on the other hand, could hold a grudge forever, as evidenced by his continued flinging of her faith in her face. She didn't understand why it bothered him as much as it did, and the times she'd asked, he'd brushed it off. Mom had mentioned once that his parents had been religious. She'd never known either set of grandparents. Her brother, Cyan, had looked up her dad's folks a handful of years ago and said they were good people, if normal. Azure could use a little good and normal in her life.

Hands in her pockets, she crossed through the tiny kitchen to the den. Her parents were stretched out in their recliners, reading. She smiled. The recliners were new, but otherwise it was a common picture of her folks from childhood. Evenings and weekend afternoons were always spent relaxed with a book or some other quiet project. It's when she'd learned to love art, both seeing it and creating it.

Azure perched on the edge of the couch. "I think I'm gonna head out."

Her mother put a bookmark between the pages of her book and set it aside. "Out where?"

"Out, out." Azure gestured vaguely. "Wherever's next."

"Is this because of your father?" Her mother reached over and slapped her dad's arm. "I told you you were too hard on her."

"No, Mom. It's fine. Dad's just saying how he feels, which is what he's always done. I'm used to it. I just think it's time. I've been here two weeks. You've got to be getting tired of company."

"You're not company, you're our daughter." Her mother frowned. "Where will you go?"

Azure shrugged. "I can make it to Albuquerque tonight. After that, I guess I'll see where the wind blows."

Her father cocked his head to the side. "Think it'll blow you back to Virginia?"

"Why would you ask that?"

"I may just be your dumb old dad, but I know a thing or two about love."

"Love? No one's said anything about love. At best we're friends." Azure shook her head. The words sounded right, but her heart screamed against them. Still, it was always better to listen to head, wasn't it? "I like Matt. He's funny and handsome and easy to be around. But he's also pushy and stubborn."

"Sounds like someone I know." Her mother grinned and glanced over at her father. "He shares your faith, too, yes?"

Azure nodded.

"Then I'd say you could do much worse. And even if you're not willing to admit to love just yet, I'd encourage you to listen to your heart and see if it doesn't line up with the things your head is also telling you." Her mother pushed down the footrest of her recliner and stood. She walked to Azure and wrapped her in a tight hug. "I'm so glad you came to see us. I love you and I'm proud of the woman you've become."

Her dad joined them, dropping a kiss on Azure's forehead as he squeezed her shoulder. "What your mother said. And...I know I give you grief about your faith. I'm sorry. I also see it makes you steadier than you used to be. For that, I'm grateful."

"Thanks, Dad. I love you both. I probably won't be home for Christmas."

"We understand." Her mother kissed her cheek. "Grab another jar or two of lotion out of the pantry on your way out. Your young man should need a refill before too much longer if it's working."

Azure chuckled as she stood and hugged both of her parents again. She had a good family. As she left, she collected the hand cream and prayed that God would continue to pursue her parents and her siblings. They needed Him. It broke her heart that they refused to see it.

After hooking the trailer to her truck, she climbed into the cab and sent her brother Cyan a quick text asking about her grandparents. Maybe if they were east of here, they'd be a good next destination.

The aspen trees had dropped all their leaves, but the drive from Albuquerque to Santa Fe was still breathtaking. She'd taken a day and browsed the numerous galleries and historic buildings in New Mexico's capital, working up her courage to call the grandparents she'd never met and ask if she could come meet them.

They'd been thrilled.

Just like Cyan said they would be.

Traveling now from Santa Fe toward Taos, her fingers itched for a paintbrush. Even the bare trees begged to be painted. A blanket of snow covered the ground, but the roads were clear. Still, Azure kept her speed just under the limit. The last thing she wanted was to take a turn and end up with her trailer pulling her down the side of a mountain. Or mesa. Whatever they were called here.

Before long, Azure drove past the iconic Saint Francis de Asis church in Rancho de Taos. She couldn't stop herself. She found a spot to park and got out, walking until she had the typical angle seen in pictures. She snapped a few on her cell—it would be a nice addition to the New Mexico series of paintings brewing in the back of her mind—and headed back to her truck. She was meeting her grandparents at the Taos Plaza, in front of Hotel La Fonda de Taos.

Butterflies danced in her stomach. Why had her parents never even tried to bridge the gap? She'd talked to her mom this morning. As usual, Mom hadn't asked too many questions—her theory that grown children didn't need parental guidance was sometimes a blessing—it had saved Azure from having to decide what to say when asked why she was looking her relatives up. Mom would probably understand, but Dad? She shook her head. That seemed unlikely.

The plaza opened up in front of her. Adobe buildings formed a square perimeter around a bandstand and seating area. There was no lush, green garden in the center like one would find in places like Savannah, though tall trees did provide some shade and greenery. There were parking spots for normal-sized vehicles in front of the shops, but nothing that would accommodate her trailer. With a frown, Azure drove a complete circuit of the square. She noticed a side street and turned, following it to a little parking lot that had space for her to pull through and take up two spots.

She grabbed her coat, hopped out of the truck, and headed back toward the hotel. At least, having driven past, she knew where to go. She was a little early, so she might just take a minute or two to peer into the galleries along the way. It never hurt to see if there were new venues for her paintings. She had the business cards of a three different gallery owners in Santa Fe who were interested in seeing what she produced in the future. As much as she loved and appreciated Rob and Crystal, diversification was necessary for artistic longevity.

A lot of the art ran to jewelry and pottery, but even those pieces sparked ideas that Azure longed to paint. If things went well with her grandparents, maybe she could hang at their place for a week or two and get those ideas out on canvas. As it was, she'd spent too much time sketching the silver squash blossoms on a belt studded with turquoise and now was in danger of being late to the hotel. Azure took a deep breath, pressed a hand to her stomach, and, with a wave to the gallery manager hurried out into the plaza toward the hotel.

Inside, Azure scanned the people sitting in clusters in the oh-so-Southwestern lobby. She didn't even know what her grandparents looked like. She had a vague notion that she'd recognize them—shouldn't she? Somehow? Maybe they'd recognize her.

Across the room, a silver-haired couple stood by the adobe fireplace that took up the corner. The man was a picture of what Azure imagined her dad would look like in forty years. That had to be them. Swallowing the lump that was suddenly in her throat, Azure strode in their direction.

"Are you the Hewitts?"

The woman grinned and glanced at the man. "We are. I wondered if that was you. Azure, yes?"

"Yes. Hi." Azure wiped her hand on her jeans, unsure. Offering to shake hands seemed rude, but a hug seemed overly familiar. "I'm not sure what to do here."

The man laughed and opened his arms. "How about a hug?"

Azure stepped into his embrace and breathed in his woodsy scent. It was the most at home she'd felt since Matt had wrapped her in his arms. Her heart panged. Would she ever stop missing him? She stepped back. "Thanks for agreeing to meet me."

"Oh, honey, we've wanted to meet you since you were born, but your mom and dad have always insisted that we keep our distance unless you sought us out. We've enjoyed getting to know your brother Cyan over the last year. We're so glad you called." Her grandmother smiled. "Why don't you call us Wayne and Betsy for now? Then, if you warm up to it later, you can switch to grandma and grandpa."

Azure chuckled and some of the tension in her chest loosened. "That'll work."

"Did you want to grab some lunch? There's a nice little Mexican place around the corner that we usually hit when we're in town. It'd be a chance for you to ask the

questions that are probably lined up in your head."
Wayne winked. "We'll let you go first."

"Lunch would be good. Thanks." Azure zipped
her coat back up. "Lead the way."

"Your brother says you're an artist. What sort?"
Betsy fell into step beside Azure as they crossed the lobby
and headed out into the plaza. Wayne walked a few steps
ahead, but his head was tilted, giving Azure the
impression that he was listening intently.

"I paint, mostly." She was never sure how much
to say. Did people want to know the different mediums
she used? Subjects she preferred? Or was the question
simply something to keep the awkward silence at bay?

"Your father used to paint." Betsy gave a small,
sad smile. "I don't imagine you have any idea about that."

Azure shook her head. Dad had never particularly
appreciated that Azure was making a living through her
art. Had he minded when her mom took lessons? She
couldn't remember. Still, he acted like Azure's success
was almost a personal affront to him in some way.
Maybe, knowing this new bit of history, it was. "No. He's
never said a word."

"Yes, well. I encouraged it, so when he left I
figured he'd leave that behind with us and everything we
stood for. We pray that someday God will bring him
back—to Himself, first of all, but to us, too."

"To Himsel—you mean God? My dad?"

Wayne stopped in front of a wooden door and
pulled it open. Pain etched lines in his face. "He doesn't
talk about us at all?"

"Not a word. If I didn't know that everyone had parents, I'd figure he sprang fully formed from a cabbage or something."

Betsy snickered but she reached for Wayne's hand. "You're mixing your mythology there, but I get your point. I'd hoped that maybe, since you and your brother reached out, maybe your dad was thawing toward us."

Azure shook her head. "He's so adamantly opposed to Jesus. I—that's why I'm on my way back east now. I'd thought I would stay with them in Arizona through Christmas, but it was too much."

"You're a believer?" Wayne held up three fingers for the hostess and they followed her to a table.

"Yeah, I am."

"Is Cyan?"

"Not that I'm aware of, no. But I'm working on him. Praying for him. Of my siblings, he's the most likely, I think, to get there." Azure flipped open the menu and scanned the offerings. Her grandparents weren't quite what she expected. Not that she'd been sure what to expect. Cyan had said they were nice, and that's about it, wanting her to discover them for herself. He'd probably known that Azure would have more in common with them as someone who loved Jesus.

"What about your dad?" Wayne reached for a chip and dunked it in the bright red salsa on the table.

Azure frowned. "What about him?"

"Do you pray for him?"

She sighed. "I try to. For him and my mom. It's hard sometimes. They're both so—"

Betsy chuckled and touched Azure's hand. "They really are. But that's why they need us to pray for them. I'm trusting God to bring our whole family to Him. Ultimately, though, as hard as it can be for those of us praying, it's their decision. God doesn't force anyone to come to Him."

Azure nodded. She knew that. So many parts of the Christian life were like that. It was probably the hardest thing for her. As someone who lived her life on the road, maps were her lifeblood. She'd sit and look at maps any time, given the chance. But God didn't hand them out with clearly marked routes. She was trying to learn to trust, to wait, and to listen for His leading. It was *hard*. Just like how God didn't force anyone to commit to Him, He also didn't stop people from going their own way when He'd prefer a different path. Had she done that when she'd left Virginia? The longer she was away from Matt, the more it seemed like she had. Well, she'd repented and she was making her way back there. Hopefully, God would redeem the mistake.

"Tell me about your ranch." Azure sipped her water. It was time to push the conversation away from her, at least a little.

Betsy and Wayne exchanged a glance before Betsy spoke. "Why don't you come out after lunch and see it for yourself?"

14

Matt cranked the wrench and set the tool aside with a sigh. He missed Azure. She'd been gone a month and his heart still ached for her. Since the incident in Atlanta, what conversations they'd had were stilted. They'd texted more than talked. She was in New Mexico visiting grandparents she'd never met until two days ago. What must that be like?

His grandparents had died two years after his parents. He had fond memories of several visits with them—both with his parents and, later, with his aunt and uncle. He couldn't picture his childhood without knowing they were there for him if he needed them. Was it any wonder Azure struggled with the idea of putting down roots? She'd never had any.

And sure, he railed against his sometimes. Even now, Uncle Jim was driving him a little crazy with the garage transition, which was why he was working on the Stingray alone on a Sunday afternoon instead of spending time with them. It didn't help that Aunt Ida was counting down the month of days left until they left on their cruise. Every day from now until they headed out of town had a long list of preparation that had to be done. Matt had tried to remind her there were only two of them, not an army. He wouldn't do that again.

He glanced over at his phone. What was Azure doing? He wanted to hear her voice. Matt sighed and reached for the thing. Pride was the only thing keeping him from calling, and that simply wasn't enough. Not anymore. He tapped her name and waited while it rang.

"Hey, Matt." Azure sounded tired.

Matt glanced at the time and frowned. Even with the time difference she ought to be awake. "Hi. Am I calling at a bad time?"

"No. We just got back from church and I was thinking of taking a nap. I was up late last night, painting."

"Isn't it a little cold for that?" He'd never thought of equating New Mexico with cold and snow, but that was exactly what Azure had told him they had. There were even several well-known skiing spots not far from her grandparents' ranch. Who knew?

Azure chuckled. "It's too cold to even be in the trailer. Wayne and Betsy put me up in one of the cabins. It's much nicer. Central heat and everything."

"Fancy." The word cabin didn't evoke heaters for Matt, but he was grateful in this case that he was wrong. "And really nice of them."

"It was. They're great. I'm more than a little bummed that I've missed out on so much time with them."

"Do you think you'll stay there a while, then?" His stomach clenched. He'd hoped she was headed back to Peacock Hill, but hadn't wanted to ask. Asking would turn to begging, and that wouldn't be positive for either of them.

She sighed. "I don't know. Maybe a week? Certainly until I get this painting finished. Although, I have an idea for another one as well, and I might like to try and get it at least started before getting back on the road."

"Where do you think you'll head, once you do leave?" It was as close as Matt was going to get to asking outright.

"I'm not sure. I—Matt?"

"Yeah?"

"If I came back to Virginia, would you be willing to see if we could pick up where we left off?"

His heart leapt in his chest. "I'd like that. A lot."

"I don't know if I'm ready to put down roots, but I'd like to try it, I think, if you're there."

Matt closed his eyes and sent up a silent prayer of thanks. He'd been committing their relationship to God every night, trying to open his hands and accept whatever God did with it. Maybe things would still end poorly between them, but if she came back, they could at least give it a stronger try. "Do you think you'll be back for Thanksgiving?"

"I'll make sure of it. Are you positive your aunt won't mind if I join your family meal?"

"She'll probably do cartwheels. She's asked about you several times. If you're worried, though, we could go up to Peacock Hill instead. I can probably convince my aunt and uncle to join what's sure to be an enormous gathering up there. In fact, if it's okay with you, I'm betting Aunt Ida will jump at the chance to see the renovations now that they're complete."

"Either way. I just want to be with you. I've missed you. I'm sorry—for leaving, for being stubborn about the thing in Atlanta, for everything. Forgive me?"

"Of course. I'm sorry I reacted so badly. I was scared, and I didn't like that you were in danger and I couldn't protect you. You matter to me, Azure." Azure's muffled yawn made him laugh. "I should let you go."

"I'm sorry. It's just—"

"Don't worry about it. You're coming home. That's all that matters. Call me later?"

"Yeah. Bye, Matt."

He punched end and tucked the phone back in his pocket before glancing at the 'Vette. Maybe it was time to call his uncle and take the old girl out for a spin.

"So. I hear Azure's headed back for Thanksgiving?" Jeremiah moved around the classroom in the basement of the church collecting Bibles.

Matt kept straightening the chairs. "Yeah."

Jeremiah paused and cocked his head. "And how does that make you feel?"

"Seriously?" Matt laughed and shook his head. "Are we girls now?"

"Women. You know at our age they prefer the term 'women' right?"

Matt shrugged, a grin spreading across his face. "My apologies, Mary."

Jeremiah snorted out a laugh. "Fine, fine. Question still stands."

Matt sighed. "Excited. Terrified. Confused. Slightly nauseous. Pick one. Or roll them all together into a hot, churning ball and drop it in my stomach."

"Really?"

Matt nodded.

"Welcome to being in love."

Love? His breath hitched. "There's no way that's what love is."

"Keep telling yourself that." Jeremiah set the stack of Bibles up on the front table before perching on it and studying Matt. "What did you think it was?"

Vague images of singing cartoon bluebirds flashed through his mind and heat crawled up his neck. He shrugged. "Not this."

Jeremiah smiled. "What are you going to do?"

"I don't—get to know her better, I guess. I mean, she was here what, a month before she took off? And yeah, okay, we've been texting and calling for another six weeks, but that's not exactly the world's longest relationship. If it can even be called a relationship. It's more like a friendship."

"With kissing."

Matt pressed his lips together. He never should've mentioned that to Jeremiah. "Yeah, well. Maybe we jumped the gun there."

Jeremiah's eyebrows lifted.

Matt sighed. How was he supposed to explain something he didn't really understand himself? "I can't help wondering if maybe she would've stayed if she wasn't freaked out about that when I told her about the garage. Maybe she thought I was somehow letting her know I expected her to settle down and be a small-town mechanic's wife."

"Were you?"

"Not really. I guess I wanted her to know that was the only future here, though. And maybe I wasn't super surprised when she left because of that."

Jeremiah shook his head. "Why do you always sell yourself short?"

"I'm not. I'm a mechanic in a small town. I just bought a garage, so it's not like that's going to change any time soon. It's who I am. And, as you pointed out not too long ago, it seems to be what God has for me. I'm working on being okay with it." Matt dropped into the beat up couch and crossed his arms. None of that had changed. Why was Azure coming back? She'd said she was willing to look at putting down roots—but was she? Really?

"What's going on in your head?" Jeremiah frowned. "It looks like you're ready to call her up and tell her to run in the opposite direction."

"Shouldn't she? I mean, come on, Jeremiah. I'm no great catch. If I were, surely someone would've been interested before now."

"Or maybe you've been waiting for the woman God has for you. Like we committed to doing in high school. Remember?"

"Yeah. It just didn't seem like it was going to be such an ordeal back then."

Jeremiah laughed. "Tell me about it." He stood and jerked his head toward the door. "Come on, let's go get a milkshake."

"Cause that makes everything better?" Matt chuckled as he lugged himself out of the couch. He needed to remember not to sit on that thing—it could eat a small country and no one would ever notice.

"Nope. But at least you'll have had some ice cream."

"There's that." Matt tucked his hands in his pockets and followed his friend out of the room. He still wasn't sold on calling what he felt for Azure love. He cared about her, sure. And he ached to spend more time with her. But love? There had to be more to love than that.

Thanksgiving was Thursday. Azure was supposed to arrive today. Matt still wasn't sure if Jeremiah was right or not. Love seemed like such a big word. Important. It wasn't something he'd ever said to someone, well, except for his parents and his aunt and uncle. That didn't count. Everyone would agree that was different. He rolled the word around in his mind. It wasn't the same jolt to his system that it used to be, but it was definitely not comfortable.

Matt checked the time again.

"You got someplace to be, boss?" Gage, his sole remaining part-time mechanic, leaned a hip on the hood of the car that had been dropped off for an oil change this morning.

"No. Why?"

"You keep checking the time." Gage's eyes lit with laughter. "Hot date tonight then?"

Matt shook his head. "Shouldn't you be working?"

Gage grinned. "Is this the only car we've got today?"

Matt nodded. "So far, yeah. So if you need to take off after you finish, you can. I guess I should go tackle the paperwork."

"We doing okay here?"

"Yeah. It's a slower time of year, you know that." Until the snow and ice started and some body work from fender benders started to roll in. "Why?"

"The garage in Waynesboro offered me full-time hours. I don't love the idea of the commute every day, but..." Gage trailed off and shrugged.

Matt swallowed. He could get along without Gage. In some ways, it'd be better not to have the extra payroll, but he'd hate it when things picked up. Still. "Do what you need to do, man. I can't promise you full-time anytime soon. I'd like to get there, eventually, but I don't have a timeline on that."

Gage frowned. "All right. I'll keep you posted."

"Thanks." Shaking his head, Matt headed into the office and stared at the pile of paperwork waiting for him. If Gage left, that would make extra room in the budget for an office manager who could also answer phones. Not that he had any leads on someone who'd want that job. Was it something Azure would even consider?

Maybe that was getting ahead of himself. First, she had to make it back to town. Then, they had to see if she could—would—stick around for more than a month. And then? Maybe then, they could talk about the feasibility of her working in the front office.

Matt blew out a breath and gave up. He grabbed his cell and dialed.

"Hey. I'm about an hour out." Azure's voice held a grin. "Want me to pick up lunch and bring it to the garage when I get to town?"

"More than anything." Matt clamped his mouth shut. That was supposed to have been his inside voice.

"I'm looking forward to seeing you, too. I got a ticket in Charlotte."

Matt winced. "Sorry."

"Yeah, well, it happens. Not a lot mind you. It's not like I have a bad driving record."

He laughed. "Good to know. I wasn't sure if we were at the 'how's your driving record' stage of our relationship."

"Oh, absolutely. So, tell me about yours."

"My driving record?"

"Yep. Or are you hiding something? Are you one of those guys insurance companies won't even talk to anymore?"

"I have insurance." He tried to put a little hint of defensiveness into his voice. He hadn't had a ticket in his life, but it was fun to play.

"Uh huh. Seriously. How bad is it? You can tell me. I told you I got a ticket, so there's nothing to be ashamed of."

"I wouldn't know, I've never had one."

"Oh, come on."

"I'm serious."

"No way. You're pushing thirty and have never had a speeding ticket. I don't know what to do with that information."

"Bask in my greatness?"

"Oh, please."

Matt grinned. "What are you going to get for lunch?"

"I don't know. Now that I'm aware of all the money you must have socked away because of all the fines you haven't had to pay, I'm thinking maybe you should buy me lunch."

"I can do that." He winced. "If Gage can hang out a little longer and mind the store. Let me ask him."

"I'm kidding. I'll bring it. Let Gage get on with whatever it is he does with his time."

That was an interesting point. What *did* Gage do with his time? He should ask. Or, if he was going to leave, maybe he shouldn't. "Can't wait to see you."

"Yeah? I might feel the same way. It's almost like I'm coming home."

"I like the sound of that."

"Thought you might. See you soon. Bye."

Matt ended the call and smiled. Coming home. Hopefully, he'd be able to convince her it was a permanent sentiment.

15

Azure pulled her truck and trailer into the parking lot of the big chain grocery store at the edge of town. She'd much rather visit one of the little shops on the main drag, but there was no place to park with the trailer still attached. So, big box store it was. On the positive side, the deli inside this particular type of store made a mean sub and, if her memory served, also had potato salad that wasn't half bad. It wasn't fancy gourmet fare, but it was tasty and filling. Those seemed like the attributes Matt would be more interested in than anything else.

She glanced to the side as she strode through the doors. She never had made it out here to check out their dumpsters in September. If she wasn't taking Matt lunch, she'd go look now, but showing up in dirty jeans didn't seem like the impression she was hoping to make. The canned orchestration of what probably used to be a pop song piped through the speakers made her cringe. Did anyone actually want to listen to that while they shopped?

Azure shook her head and made a bee line for the deli. Get lunch and get out. Come back another day to see what their dumpsters were like. Maybe Matt would come with her. She grinned. Now that was a thought.

She added two sodas from the mini fridge by the checkout to her order and waved off the plastic bag before jogging back out to the truck. She was so close to Matt now, she couldn't handle any more delay.

The garage bay doors were both open and empty when she turned into the garage lot. She parked, grabbed the food, and hopped down from her truck. She took a deep breath and the jangling of her nerve endings calmed slightly. It's just Matt.

The glass door to the little sitting and reception area opened and Matt stepped out, a big grin on his face. "You're here."

"I am."

He reached for the sandwiches. "Let me help you with that. It's really good to see you."

She paused for a minute to drink him in. The mental pictures she'd studied late at night when she couldn't sleep had nothing on the real thing. She followed him into the building and set the rest of the food down on the desk where the cash register sat, then she turned and launched herself at him, flinging her arms around his waist and burying her head into his shoulder. "I missed you."

Matt staggered back a step, laughing. He tossed the sandwiches toward the desk before wrapping his arms around her to hold her in place. "Yeah? Me too."

She tilted her face up and smiled. "I'm so glad."

He chuckled and tightened his grip. "You're back now."

"I am." It did funny things to her belly when she thought through the idea of home, but they weren't bad. Just different. Seeing her parents and their new house, she'd realized something she'd always taken for granted. Home didn't mean a place, it was people. For her, those people—and therefore her home—had been transient. But her parents were just as at home in their house than they'd been in the bus when she'd been growing up. Because they were together. That realization had realigned something in her heart and she'd known what she needed to do. She eased back. "I'm also hungry."

"Then let's eat." Matt hesitated a moment before letting her go. "We can sit in here or in the office. It's a little roomier out here."

"Out here it is, then." She slipped behind the desk and plopped into the chair. "I got subs—roast beef with everything—and some potato salad."

His stomach grumbled loud enough she could hear it.

Azure laughed. "I'll take that as approval."

Matt dragged a chair over and nodded. "Absolutely. Do you have forks? I can probably dig some up if I need to."

She tugged two plastic forks out of the wrapper of one of the sandwiches and handed it to him. "No plates though. I didn't think you'd mind just digging in the tub for the potato salad?"

"Hmm. Girl cooties."

"Seriously?"

"Nope." He grinned. "I was hoping I might contract a few cooties another way later."

Heat burned across her cheeks. He hadn't kissed her hello and she'd been determined to follow his lead. After all, she'd been the one to leave. If he needed them to back up or, worst case scenario, start over, she'd been planning to find a way to be okay with it. But she'd be a lot happier to skip all that. She cleared her throat. "That can probably be arranged."

"Tell me about your paintings. Did you take pictures?" Matt unwrapped his sub and took a huge bite.

"I always take pictures. You really want to see them?"

He nodded.

She wiped her fingers on a napkin and dug her phone out of her pocket. She opened her photo gallery and slid it across to Matt. It was nice of him to ask, but he really didn't have to pretend he was interested. It wasn't like she cared a ton about cars. Sure, she and her dad had refurbished the Studebaker, but that was a one-time thing. Mostly. She did enjoy tinkering now and then. "You don't have to—"

"Shh." Matt studied the first photo, his lips pursed. After a moment, he swiped to the next. His eyes widened. "This is a gorgeous one of the house. You need to show it to Deidre."

Azure winced. "I kind of don't want to. It already sold."

"I'm not surprised. Think you could do something similar? Not like replicating this one—just another one of the house? It'd make a killer wedding gift."

Wedding gift. Why hadn't she thought of that? She hadn't been able to come up with any compelling reason to hang on to it when she wasn't sure Deidre would want it. "You're sure she'd like something like that?"

"Since she's not blind or stupid, yes." He swiped to the next photo and shook his head.

"What?" Azure craned her neck to see which one he was on. What was wrong with it?

"You have an amazing talent."

Heat flooded her face. It was nice to hear from someone whose opinion mattered to her. She appreciated Rob and Crystal's encouragement, and her mom was always pleasant about her work, but this was different somehow. "Thank you."

Matt swiped to the next photo and grinned. "Are these your grandparents?"

"Oh. Ha, yeah. That's the end of the art pictures." She reached for the phone.

"You look a bit like your grandma. Around the eyes, mostly."

Did she? Azure studied the photo and nodded. Now that he pointed it out, she could see it. "I guess I do. Thanks again. It was weird hanging out with them, knowing we were related, but not having a lifetime of common ground and shared memories. I liked them, but it felt like getting to know a couple at church more than my grandparents."

"I can see that. Sort of. I mean, other than knowing up here," he tapped his forehead, "that they're your grandparents, there's nothing else there to build on. Yet."

"Yet. I like that. Their ranch is lovely, I'd like to visit again. Although, they were talking about retiring. I'm not sure what that means. It didn't seem like it was my place to ask, you know? I didn't want them to think I was angling for any kind of handout or something like that." Azure shrugged. "It was still a good visit."

"I'm glad you got to meet them."

It was too bad he hadn't been there with her. She reached across the table and touched his hand. She needed the contact. Matt flipped his hand over and threaded his fingers through hers. Azure smiled.

"Are you parking out behind Peacock Hill again?"

Azure shook her head. "It's too cold. The trailer isn't set up for winter temperatures."

"Winter? It's fall." Matt chuckled. "But I'll admit to not wanting to camp in this weather myself."

"Exactly. So I asked Deidre if the offer of a room was still available. She said absolutely. I've gotten a little more used to living inside something other than my little space since Atlanta. Turns out some of the more deserted campgrounds aren't as safe as they always used to seem."

He nodded.

"No, I told you so?"

"Don't see the point. It was never about being right. It was always about you being safe. I care about you, Azure. A lot."

Her heart warmed. It wasn't a declaration of love, but it was heading in the right direction. She wasn't ready for that sort of announcement anyway. And if the little twinge of disappointment didn't ease, she'd keep telling herself that until she believed it.

Deidre squealed and ran down the steps, throwing her arms around Azure and giving her a hard hug. For a petite woman, Deidre packed a punch.

Azure laughed and patted Deidre's back. "If I'd known you'd be this excited to see me, I would've come back sooner."

"Please." Deidre stepped back with a grin. "I know it wasn't *me* that got you back here. But I'm still glad you are. You'll stay for the wedding at least, right?"

Azure nodded. At this point, she had no plans to leave again for the foreseeable future. She was pretty sure developing roots required sticking around long enough for them to have a chance to dig down into the soil. Another month, give or take a week, wasn't exactly a long time. "Wouldn't miss it for the world. You're sure you don't mind if I set up and paint?"

"Not if you don't drip on the floor." Deidre grinned. "You're not going to be in the way at all. We're finished inside. I keep trying to think of something I've missed, but Sean is right. We're ready to open. I'm terrified."

Azure couldn't really even imagine. From what she gathered, Deidre had walked away from a solid business up near D.C. to buy and renovate Peacock Hill in order to turn it into not only her home, but a wedding venue and retreat center. "What's Claire say?"

"That we should've started taking reservations in September and that if we're not careful, our first spring and summer are going to be miserable failures because brides book way more in advance than we're allowing them by opening now."

"She's such an optimist."

Deidre laughed. "Yeah, she really is. But I also know she's not wrong. I've been praying hard that God wouldn't let my foot-dragging cripple our shot before we have a chance to really get going. Can I help you with bags or something? It's chilly out here."

Azure shook her head. "Not yet. I wanted to make sure you were alright with me parking the trailer here in front. Or was there somewhere else?"

"I'm fine with over by those cedars." Deidre pointed to a stand of trees off to the side a little, but still in the front. "It'll be out of the way there but still accessible."

"Perfect. I'll get it settled and then drag some stuff in. Second floor?"

"Yeah. Any room other than Anna's is yours. Take two if you need the space."

"Do you see what I'm used to living in?" Azure chuckled and hopped back into her truck, turning to meet Deidre's eyes. "I really appreciate you taking me in."

"Even if you weren't here for Matt, I'd do it. The fact that you are just makes it sweeter. He's a good guy."

She nodded. Was she here for Matt? It wasn't how she'd phrase it, but it also wasn't completely wrong. Something about it rubbed her wrong. She sighed and circled around so she could back the trailer into the little area Deidre had indicated. She unhooked the trailer from the truck and grabbed the overnight bag and small parcel of art supplies she'd gotten together after lunch with Matt. She'd start working on the painting for Deidre and Jeremiah's wedding right away, but after that? She had plenty of ideas, but she couldn't paint all day every day. She'd go crazy. Maybe Deidre had some odd jobs she could tackle. Or some place in town. One thing was clear, she'd need more than painting to help her establish those roots.

16

Matt slid out from the backseat of his aunt and uncle's car and breathed in. There was something about the mountain air in fall. It held a tang of wood smoke and leaves, and it settled his churning gut.

"Grab the green bean casserole and rolls out of the trunk, would you Matt?" Aunt Ida climbed out of the passenger seat and turned to look at the house. "It's good to see the place cleaned up again. She's a beauty, isn't she?"

Uncle Jim slung his arm around Ida's shoulders and pulled her close. "It is. It'll be better to see the inside. Wonder if it still looks like we remember it?"

Matt got the food out of the trunk and nodded toward the stairs. "Let's go in and find out."

Deidre had put up a wreath of bright orange and yellow leaves and a hay bale and corn stalks made a little tableau to the right of the front door. It was a homey touch that said thanksgiving. Matt smiled. Deidre had a knack of making everyone feel at home here at Peacock Hill. It never felt like an imposing mansion, and it very easily could've.

Matt knocked and pulled open the door, calling out as he did so. "It's the Pattersons."

Uncle Jim chuckled as he gestured for Ida to go through the door first.

Aunt Ida balked. "We can't just walk in."

"Sure we can. Go on. Deidre knows we're coming and my arm is about to burn to a crisp holding this casserole. How is it staying so hot?"

"Oh, don't be such a baby." Aunt Ida frowned and grabbed the dish from Matt before she stalked into the entry hall.

"Well, that got her moving, at least." Uncle Jim rolled his eyes. "But it's not going to win you any points."

Matt shrugged. He knew the way around Aunt Ida, she was too much his mom to stay mad for long. He came to stand beside her and kissed her cheek. "Let me get that. You go poke around."

"I couldn't. I—can I really?"

"Of course you can." Deidre came into the foyer from the direction of the kitchen and dining room. "Or I can take you around. But you're more than welcome to just wander. Upstairs, if a door's closed, knock first though. I'd hate for you to walk in on Duncan before he has a shirt on."

Uncle Jim chuckled. "I'll be sure to keep an eye on her, then, I'd hate for your brother to make a play for my girl."

Ida's cheeks pinked. "Oh, honestly, Jim. That boy's half my age."

"At least," Matt muttered.

"I heard you, Matthew." Ida pinned him with a glare. "However, seeing as it's Thanksgiving, I'll let it slide. Just this once." She glanced at Deidre. "You really don't mind if we poke around?"

Deidre grinned. "Not at all. We'll serve lunch in about a half an hour."

Uncle Jim and Aunt Ida wandered into the front parlor and Matt shook his head. "She's been dying to see the inside since you started fixing things up."

"Well, hopefully it'll pass muster." Deidre jerked her head toward the kitchen. "Why don't you bring the food this way and then you can find someplace to relax. I think Jeremiah has the TV on in the peacock room."

"The peacock room?" Every room in the house had at least one peacock in it. How was he supposed to know which was which?

"Back parlor? Or I guess it was maybe called the music room? It's the one with all the peacocks carved into the wood. We made it sort of a TV lounge for guests. The front parlor will just be for gatherings and conversation, nothing electric in there but the lights. And of course both rooms are easily cleared to be used for smaller, indoor weddings or overflow reception space."

Matt nodded as he stepped into the kitchen. Deidre seemed nervous. It was a lot, turning a place like this into a wedding venue *and* retreat center. Conventional wisdom would probably suggest she choose one or the other, and maybe over time it would settle into that, but it seemed to Matt that having options was a good thing.

He set the casserole and basket of rolls on the counter and turned, his gaze landing on Azure. His whole body seemed to get lighter.

"There you are." Azure slipped off the stool at the kitchen table and crossed to him. She lifted her chin and brushed her lips across his. "I was wondering when you'd get here."

Deidre cleared her throat. "I think that's my cue. If the oven time goes off, come find me, would you?"

"You don't have to—" The swinging kitchen door cut off Matt's objection. "Maybe she did."

Azure rested her head on his shoulder. "I'm not complaining. I haven't seen you since I got back in town."

He kissed the top of her head. "It's only been two days. I figured you'd be busy getting settled."

"I guess I was." She sighed. "I got a start on the painting you mentioned. Maybe after lunch we can sneak upstairs and I can show you. I want to make sure it's what you had in mind."

Matt frowned slightly. The hesitation in her voice wasn't typical. Usually, Azure was confident about her art. About everything. "If you're painting it, it's going to be perfect. What's wrong?"

She shrugged and stepped out of his embrace, pacing the width of the kitchen. "I don't know. I can't paint all day every day. I had one day of it yesterday and I'm already going stir crazy. Sure, I made good progress and I could probably churn out the art, but..."

"But?" Matt held out a hand.

Azure took it and squeezed gently. "I think I'd run out of juice. What if I can't come up with any more ideas to paint? Or if by painting so much I lose my touch and no one wants to buy them? I've always supplemented my income with little jobs here and there—like the one here. I don't think I can be a full-time artist. I'm not sure I want to."

He fought the urge to grin. "Well, I might have a solution. I've been praying about finding someone to handle the front office end of things at the garage. Answer the phones, help with paperwork, and call delinquent accounts, that sort of thing. I've been working it in as I can, but with Gage and Uncle Jim leaving, I'm the only mechanic. We're not swamped with work. If we were, I could offer Gage full-time hours and he wouldn't be leaving. Since he is, though, I have a little more wiggle room in the budget for someone to do the phones and stuff. I was hoping that someone might be you, but I didn't want to ask."

"Why not?"

"Your art is amazing. It's obvious, to me at least, that it's what you're supposed to do. I didn't want you to think I was trying to take you away from that, or that I didn't understand that." Maybe it sounded a little lame, but he didn't know how else to explain how much he admired her talent.

"I—" The oven timer buzzed, cutting her off.

"I'll go find Deidre." He squeezed her hand before letting go. "Think about it, okay?"

Azure nodded.

Belly full, Matt lounged on one of the extra-wide chairs Deidre had ordered for the TV area. Azure was snuggled next to him, sharing the space. It was about as perfect as Matt could imagine things being. His friends were scattered around the room alone or in pairs, chatting about this or that, with the football game droning quietly in the background. Even Aunt Ida and Uncle Jim looked comfortable on the sofa next to him.

Aunt Ida shifted and touched Uncle Jim's knee. "We should get going and leave the young people to their afternoon."

Jim nodded and lurched to his feet before turning and offering his hand to his wife. "That's a good plan. Matt, can you get a ride home?"

"I'll bring him home." Azure smiled up at him and his insides warmed.

"All right then." Aunt Ida nodded. She glanced over at Deidre. "Thank you for including us, you put together a lovely meal."

Deidre stood. "You're very welcome. I'm glad you could make it. I'd hoped my parents would be able to make the trip down, but they decided to go on a cruise instead."

Ida laughed. "That's the prerogative of empty nesters. We're doing that to Matt for Christmas this year, but I think he'll be all right."

His heart clutched. He somehow hadn't really put it together that they'd be gone for Christmas. Of course, he'd known the dates of their vacation, but the reality hadn't sunk in. He glanced around at the gathering of friends who were, effectively, also family. "Yeah, I guess I will. But I'll miss you."

"We'll send you a post card." Ida leaned over and kissed his cheek. After a moment, she laid her hand on Azure's shoulder. "I trust you'll still be here when we get back?"

Azure visibly swallowed. "That's the plan, yes."

"Good. You're good for him. And I think he's good for you. I had my doubts, as you know, but seeing how Matt is when you're around—and how he is when you're not—I think the former is a better situation." Aunt Ida smiled. "I've never been one who's minded admitting when she's wrong."

Uncle Jim snorted.

Ida laughed and swatted his arm. "Let's get on home. Thanks again."

"I'll walk you out. I really do appreciate you coming." Deidre tagged along with Matt's aunt and uncle.

"Stamp of approval there in front of everyone. Nice going." Jeremiah wiggled his eyebrows. "Are there wedding bells in the future?"

Claire made a disgusted sound. "Probably. It's good Dee decided to make this place a wedding venue, people come here, sneeze, and fall in love."

"Feeling left out?" Duncan crossed the room and dropped into his sister's lap before planting a noisy kiss on her cheek. "I still love you."

Claire rolled her eyes and shoved at him. "Get off. You weigh a ton. Did you know you were marrying an elephant, Anna?"

Anna laughed. "I didn't, no. I'll be sure we stock up on peanuts."

"How are the renovations on the cottage going?" Matt ran his hand along Azure's arm. Duncan and Anna were getting their future home in order, though they hadn't yet set a wedding date. Deidre was already living in the basement apartment that would be hers and Jeremiah's once they tied the knot. He pictured the little apartment over his aunt and uncle's garage. It wasn't really the kind of place a man took his new bride. Sure, it'd work in a pinch—it had four walls and a roof. But, if nothing else, it was less than a stone's throw from Aunt Ida, and that was not exactly a recipe for romance. Azure's elbow dug into his side. Clearly he'd missed a question. "Sorry. What?"

Duncan chuckled. "I asked if you wanted to walk out and see. We're practically ready to move in furniture."

"That's fast." Matt shook his head. "Not as much to do as you thought?"

"What'd I miss?" Deidre came back and settled next to Jeremiah. "I like your aunt and uncle."

"Thanks. I mostly do, too." Matt grinned. "Duncan was offering tours of the cottage. I could use a walk. What about you, Azure?"

She shrugged. "Sure. Claire? Anna?"

"I'll come." Claire stood. "Then maybe I'll go spend some time on the website. It's basically ready, but there are some tweaks that would make it better."

"It's Thanksgiving." Deidre frowned. "Don't work on Thanksgiving."

Claire shrugged. "Nothing else to do. It's fine. In fact, I'll pass on the tour and just get started on that now. It really was a nice meal though, Dee. Thanks."

Matt watched Claire leave. "What's up with her?"

Deidre sighed. "I think I know, but it's not for me to say. Why don't you go take your tour, I'll go talk to Claire. Or try to."

Jeremiah looked between the group standing and Deidre. "Where can I help?"

"You don't want to see the cottage?" Deidre frowned.

"I went by this morning with Duncan while everyone was cooking. Also, why did you get credit for the meal when Claire did almost all the cooking?"

Deidre shrugged. "It's what she wanted. I did help."

"I know you did, babe, sorry." Jeremiah grabbed Deidre's hand and pulled her onto his lap. "I'm proud of you."

"Oh, whatever." She pushed against his chest, but his arms locked around her.

"I think that's our cue. Everyone touring the cottage, with me." Duncan waved his arm and headed toward the door.

Chuckling, Matt helped Azure up out of the chair and followed. He slung his arm over her shoulders as they walked, listening to Anna and Duncan chatter about the few details yet to be finished on their new place. "It's too bad Danny couldn't make it. He always manages to cheer Claire up."

Azure snorted. "Men are idiots."

"Wait. What? Does that include me?"

Azure nodded.

"What did I miss?"

17

Azure bounced a little on the rolling chair behind the desk in the garage's office-slash-waiting room. It wasn't the most comfortable thing in the universe, but it'd do. Matt had moved things around so she could set up her easel and spend some time painting every day if she wanted.

Matt came in, wiping his hands with a rag. "So, what do you think?"

"It's great. You're sure you don't mind if I paint if there's a lull?"

"I'm sure. And it's not if, it's when. That's one of the reasons I've hesitated to advertise the position. It's not really full-time work, despite needing a body here full-time."

She laughed. "It's the ideal job for someone with other stuff they want to do, then. I'll try not to mess it up."

"I'm not sure that's possible, honestly. I've been doing such a haphazard job at it for the last ten months you can only be an improvement. If you need something, just holler."

"I will." She patted the small stack of folders on the desk. "You wanted me to start with these, right?"

He nodded. "Those are the most overdue. They've all been contacted within the last six weeks, but I've found with them that an extra nudge is always needed. For one I may end up having to see if the Sheriff can swing by, but maybe we can avoid that this time."

"Seriously? Why do you still service their cars?"

He sighed. "Small towns can be tricky. They're good people. They just seem to always have more month than money. They need the cars, though, to get to work to have even as much money as they are getting. So I feel like I'm helping out, and if they really can't pay, we can work something out."

He was soft-hearted. She'd seen hints of it here and there, but Azure hadn't realized the depth. "Is there wiggle room in the amount owed?"

"Not really." Matt flipped through the stack and set two folders aside, tapping them. "These are the two that fall into the category I just described. I pretty much just charge them for parts already. I try to make sure I do the work so I don't have to tack on some kind of labor in order to make a paycheck. But let me know what they say, and we can try and figure it out if we need to."

"Just these two?"

Matt scanned the names on the other folders and nodded. "Yeah. The rest of them are just lazy about their bills. A good nudge generally gets the money. It's not a matter of them not having it."

She didn't understand how this was an acceptable practice, but maybe it was just a part of small-town life. Moving around like she had her whole life, bills were to be dealt with immediately. Usually in cash. That way there was nothing hanging over them when it was time to move on.

"You okay?"

"Yeah. It's not something I've done before, but I should be able to manage. I like people, generally."

He grinned. "There you go. I'll get back to the alignment I'm working on, then. Come get me if you need something. Or if you just want to say hi."

She chuckled, her insides warming as he leaned across the desk and brushed a kiss over her lips. Azure watched as he ambled back into the garage bay and smiled. She might have only been back in Virginia for two weeks, but it was right. For the first time in a long time, there was nothing calling to her from someplace else.

She was exactly where she wanted to be.

Azure wandered into the kitchen at Peacock Hill. She'd eaten dinner, but she hadn't been able to settle up in her room, so she figured a snack might be just the thing. Everyone else was at church. They'd invited her along, but...it just wasn't her thing. Did she have to become one of those people who were there every time the doors were open? It was odd enough going every Sunday for service and a small group. Maybe, in time, she'd adjust. But for now, the quiet was nice.

Sort of.

Shaking her head, she pulled open the fridge and frowned at the contents. Nothing called to her. She grabbed the jar of strawberry jelly and closed the door. PB&J it was.

"Hey."

Azure startled, almost losing her grip on the jelly, and turned. "Claire. Hi. I thought you were at church too."

"Not tonight. I..." Claire hunched her shoulders. "Just couldn't get up the oomph to go."

"Danny?"

Claire frowned. "What do you mean?"

"He's dating that girl—what's her name? He was talking about it on Sunday."

"Yeah, well. Whatever."

Azure shook her head and pulled out two slices of bread. She glanced at Claire. "Want a sandwich?"

"You know what? Sure. Thanks." Claire flopped into a chair at the kitchen table with a sigh. "Is he blind? Is that the problem?"

"Clueless, most likely. Seems like that's common for men."

Claire snorted. "Oh, sure. Matt was tripping over his tongue every time you took a breath from the very beginning."

Had he been? They'd hit it off, certainly, but had he been that interested? Even now, she wasn't sure exactly what his feelings for her were. Granted, after she'd run off, he was probably waiting to see if she was serious about sticking around. Did that mean it was up to her to move things along? She spread peanut butter on the bread. "Hmm. And he's always just been friendly?"

"We flirt. He doesn't seem to realize I'm serious about it though. And it's not like I flirt with everyone."

"So back to clueless."

Claire's laugh was hollow. "I guess. It doesn't matter. It's not like I don't have stuff to do. I mean, we're booking up pretty quickly now that Deidre's given the okay for us to start taking reservations. There's plenty of work to be done. I probably don't have time for a relationship."

Azure spread jelly and flipped the top slices of bread onto the sandwiches. "Uh huh. But it makes life a lot nicer."

Claire took a plate from Azure and nodded. "Yeah, that's the truth."

Azure sat across from Claire and studied her sandwich. "Have you thought about asking him out? We're allowed to do that these days you know."

"Thought about it, decided not to."

"Why?"

Claire tore a piece off her sandwich and popped it into her mouth. "Mostly because I don't think I could handle him saying no. And I'm pretty sure he would. We hang out, and we usually end up paired when pairing has to happen—although sometimes I'd get paired with Matt before you. But I'm reasonably certain he sees me as a friend or an honorary little sister. I don't think I have the skills to change that."

Azure nodded. "So, it's weird for me to ask this. Or at least it's a little weird to me, because it's not what I'd normally ask, but I'm trying to be better at it in my own life, so I figure other people maybe struggle with it, too."

Claire gave a short laugh. "Got it. Weird question. Let's go."

Could she bungle this any more than she already was? Probably not. Just jump in and go. She took a deep breath. "Are you praying about it?"

"Oh. That." Claire took another bite of her sandwich and sighed. "Sort of."

"How do you sort of pray about something?"

"I just kind of tack Danny on at the end of my prayer before bed and then quickly gloss it over with asking for God's will and then say amen."

How many of those sorts of prayers had Azure made since she'd become a believer? Too many to count. It was still her tendency, if she wasn't careful. "I think, sometimes, it's easy to know in our heads that we're supposed to pray but not to really believe that it does any good. I know that's something I struggle with. I want to believe it matters—but how many people are there on Earth and God's supposed to care that I'm not sure where I should spend my winter?"

"Exactly."

"Except." Azure wiped her fingers and dragged her cell phone out of her pocket. She tapped open her Bible app and squeezed her eyes closed. What was the reference? She'd just read it yesterday morning. "I think it's in Luke? Jesus talks about the ravens and the flowers and how God cares about them, so of course He cares about us. And then in both Ephesians and Philippians, Paul makes it clear that God wants us to bring our concerns and requests to Him."

Claire nodded. "I know all that. I grew up in the church. It doesn't make it any easier to feel like He's listening."

"There's a lot about being a Christian that isn't easy. I'm trying to do better praying about that stuff, too."

"Yeah, I guess."

This was so far outside her comfort zone. Azure's heart hammered in her chest. "Um. If you wanted, I could pray with you about it."

"Would you?"

"Sure. Maybe you could pray for me and Matt?"

"Things aren't going well?"

Azure set her phone aside. "No, they are. I just— I'm scared. Settling down in a small town is completely foreign to me. How do I know if I'm doing it right?"

Claire laughed. "I'm not sure there's a right way to be in a small town. Or maybe I don't know either. The D.C. area is a far cry from here—and yet, I can't imagine going back. The beauty—and hardship—of a small town is the people. So to do it right you just have to be friendly, which means you're doing great."

Azure smiled. "I don't want to let Matt down."

"You're in love."

Love? She shook her head. "No. Of course not. It's much too soon for that. I like him. A lot. And I care for him, a ton. But love?"

"Trust me. If you're worried about letting him down because you don't fit into his town? You're in love. I've seen it happen enough around here in the last year, I recognize the signs." Claire stood and dumped the uneaten half of her sandwich into the trash. "Thanks, Azure."

"Anytime. Keep me posted about Danny."

Claire snorted. "Sure. But don't hold your breath."

Azure sighed and looked back at her half-eaten sandwich. She took another bite and chewed thoughtfully.

Love.

It wasn't quite like an itchy, ill-fitting sweater, but it made her hands sweat.

Maybe it was supposed to.

"You should sit down." Jeremiah grabbed Deidre's hand as she rushed past where he lounged on a couch in the TV room. "What's up with you tonight?"

"I don't know." Deidre perched on the edge of the couch, her knee jiggling. "I can't settle."

Azure chuckled. The two of them looked good together, even with Deidre being uncharacteristically edgy. "Wedding jitters? You're what, two weeks out?"

"Three." Deidre frowned. "Maybe that's it. I think everything's set though. It's set, right Claire?"

Claire set aside her e-reader. "What?"

"The wedding? It's all set, right? You haven't told me anything else I need to do, so I was assuming it was all handled." Deidre reached for Jeremiah's hand. "Please tell me it's handled."

"It's handled." Claire reached for her book again. "Haven't you been reading the daily emails Sean sends?"

"Daily?" Azure shifted so she could see out the door and into the foyer a little better. Where was Matt? He'd said he couldn't make dinner, but that he'd for sure be in time for the movie. "That seems excessive."

"And yet there are brides who apparently don't know if they're ready." Claire gestured to Deidre. "So maybe it isn't as excessive as it seems."

Azure smiled. That was fair enough. "Maybe you should scroll through those emails to help you settle."

"It's not that."

Jeremiah frowned at his fiancée. "Then what is it?"

"I don't know. Let's just start the movie. I'll be fine." Deidre scooted back on the sofa and tucked herself under Jeremiah's arm. "Where's Matt?"

Azure shrugged. "I'm not sure. He said he'd be here by now. I texted him, but haven't heard back. I'm sure it's fine. We can start. Maybe I'll give him a quick call."

Danny snorted. "If he's fine, why are you bugging him? Seriously, women make life more complicated than it needs to be."

"Really? That's where you're going with that? Is it so bad that Azure cares about Matt and is concerned?" Claire shook her head, an expression of disgust on her face. "No wonder you don't date the same person for long, the minute she starts to think you have a relationship, you probably run in the other direction."

"Wait. How did this get to be about me?" Danny threw his hands in the air. "What did I do?"

Laughing, Azure stood. "I'm going to make that call. If you want to go ahead and start the flick, go for it. I won't be long."

She stepped out into the foyer and toward the front of the house. Moving to the side of the door, she looked out at the nearly-dark yard. No sign of Matt's truck, though a few deer wandered in the large lawn that stretched out along the long driveway that led toward the road that would take someone into town.

Azure tapped Matt's photo on her phone and waited while it rang.

"Hey, babe. I don't think I'm going to make it. I was going to call you in another couple of minutes when I got this last car hooked up. Big accident out on the highway and all the tow trucks got brought in. It looks bad."

Her stomach sank. "Are you okay?"

"Yeah. I'm okay, crashes like this are always hard. Looks like teenagers playing leap frog, or maybe texting. Either way, there were three ambulances, and from what I'm looking at on the road, it seems likely at least one person didn't make it."

"Oh, gosh. That's horrible. Be safe, okay?"

"Of course. I'm really sorry I'm missing the movie. You're okay there by yourself?"

Sweet man. Her hesitancy to hang out with his friends had dissipated before she left in October, now that she was back, they were like family. "I'm good. I'm just missing snuggling with you in the big chair."

"Yeah, I'd been looking forward to that too. Look, I gotta run, but tomorrow I figured I'd close at noon if we didn't get anything major in the morning. We could drive up to Charlottesville and see some of the Christmas lights, maybe Monticello all decked up?"

"I'd like that. You know where to find me." Azure hesitated before adding. "Love you. Good night."

She tucked the phone into her pocket before wandering back into the TV lounge. The movie was on the big screen. Jeremiah and Deidre was cuddled together on the couch. Claire sat with her arms crossed, obviously ignoring everyone else in the room. Notably Danny, if Azure's guess was right. That man. Azure was tempted to give him a swift kick in the rear end for his cluelessness. Of course, it wasn't likely Claire would appreciate it, but still, he was frustrating. It didn't seem possible that he really didn't understand how much Claire liked him.

Duncan and Anna had decided to go out, so they'd missed all the drama.

Deidre glanced up. "Everything okay?"

"There's a big accident on the highway. Matt said he's not going to make it." Suddenly, the prospect of a movie didn't appeal like it had before dinner. No one would miss her if she headed up to her room. She had books on her e-reader, or she could head to bed early. Extra sleep was never a bad idea. If it gave her more time to dream about the future with Matt, well, that was even better. "I think I'm going to call it a night."

18

Christmas was five days away. Matt scraped the last bit of lotion out of the jar and rubbed it into his hands. It helped. It wasn't perfect, but it was definitely an improvement. He needed to remember to ask Azure where he could get more. She'd given him the website on her note, but he hadn't been able to find it when he looked for it last week. Probably had thrown it out in a mad fit of cleaning before she came over.

He smiled. They spent so much time together these days and he loved every minute of it. She was there at the garage during the day and most nights they had dinner together and hung out either at his place or up at Peacock Hill. She still wasn't sold on Wednesday nights at church, but that was a small thing in the overall scheme. Maybe when they started back up after the three-week break they took over Christmas and New Year's she'd be willing to try it again.

The door to his apartment swung open and Azure poked her head in. "Knock, knock."

"Hey. I was just thinking about you." He crossed the room and pulled her close, lowering his head to brush his lips across hers. "I thought you were putting your feet up and streaming some girly movie tonight."

"Still on the schedule. Probably. But I got a call on the way home and I wanted to run it by you."

"Yeah? Okay. What's up?" Taking her hand in his, he pulled her over to the couch.

"Rob called. He runs the gallery in Atlanta?"

Matt nodded.

"Anyway, since I've had so much more time to paint lately, I sent him photos of the three new canvasses I have ready."

"Not the one of the house for Deidre, right?"

Azure laughed. "No. Of course not. Actually, I have that down in the truck. I thought maybe you could keep it here so she doesn't accidentally stumble across it."

"Sure. So, Rob?"

"Rob wants the paintings. He's already sold the ones I took down in October and he has two different clients who've asked him to let them know anytime I send in something new."

Matt grinned. "That's incredible. I'm proud of you."

Azure's face lit. "Thanks. That means a lot. So here's the thing...he wants me to bring the paintings down this week and meet the clients. And I kind of feel like I should—I mean, it's a great opportunity and it's kind of a bad plan to blow them off when they're behind my ability to buy groceries and gas."

Matt struggled to keep his mouth shut while he flipped through possible responses. Her art wasn't the only thing supporting her now. Sure, it was probably more lucrative in lumps, but the paycheck from the garage was steady and not dependent on the whims of collectors. He loved her art—she had an incredible talent and he was the first to champion it. But... "It's Christmas."

"Oh, well sure. I'll hang out with Rob and Crystal and their kids for Christmas and then head back. I should still be back for Deidre and Jeremiah's wedding, no problem. I mostly wanted to be sure you'd be okay with me not being at the garage. You said you were shortening hours, but still needed to be available for emergencies."

"Can I ask you something?"

"Always."

She really didn't get it at all, did she? "Two weeks ago, the night I missed the movie because of the accident?"

"Yeah?"

"You said 'love you' before you hung up. Was that just reflex?" Matt had been waiting for the right time to mention it. Or to just tell her how he felt. But it had never seemed right. Or, when the moment would get close, something would come up. So he'd set it aside—or tried to. But now? When she was talking about zipping off again over Christmas without appearing to realize that wasn't what people in relationships did? He had to ask. Even if he didn't like the answer.

Pink tinged her cheeks. "No. It wasn't a reflex. I didn't realize you heard me. Why didn't you say something?"

"I was trying to figure out what you meant."

She drew her eyebrows together. "What I meant? I meant I love you, Matthew Patterson. Because I do."

Matt's heart hammered in his chest. He nodded.

"Now's a good time to tell me you love me, too." Azure clasped her hands together in her lap, her eyes searching his face. "You do, right?"

"I do. But," he paused and cleared his throat, "now I'm not sure it's the best idea."

Her face went blank and she blinked. "You're not sure...what does that mean?"

"It means you're taking off again and I don't know what to do with that." Matt stood and paced across the room. "At Christmas, too, like it's no big deal. You want to go to Atlanta for a week, so off you go without any thought for how that's going to affect the people in your life. Like, oh, let me see, the man you say you love. It's *Christmas*. You don't ask me, you just tell me this is how it is. You can't wait and go another time?"

"Rob's got a little thing at the gallery planned for Friday so no, I can't go another time. I need to go now, and I don't appreciate you suggesting that I don't have the freedom to do just that." Now Azure stood, her arms crossed. "And I don't see what me needing to do this has to do with being in love with you. Except that maybe that last thing shows bad judgment on my part."

Her words sliced through his heart and he stiffened. "Maybe it does. By all means, don't let me keep you. I'm sure you have some packing to do. I wouldn't want to get in your way."

Azure took a deep breath and opened her mouth. She snapped it shut and glared at him before turning on her heel and storming out. He listened as she stomped down the stairs and her truck roared to life.

As his heart cracked into pieces, Matt slid back onto the couch. His eyes burned. His parents had left him so they could have a weekend away, and they'd been killed. His aunt and uncle had left him, because they needed adventure. Now Azure was gone because random strangers who liked her art asked her to. Why didn't anyone who claimed to love him ever feel like staying?

"Knock, knock."

Matt slid out from under the car he was working on and forced a smile for Deidre. "I know you don't need another safety inspection."

"No. But I did have this for you." Deidre chuckled and held out a jar.

"It's like deja vu."

"All over again." Deidre's eyes clouded. "Are you okay?"

He stood, took the jar and frowned at it, and walked over to the workbench. Setting the jar down, he turned and leaned against the table. "Not really. Imagine I will be at some point."

"Matt."

"Just don't, okay?" He sighed and reached for a rag to wipe his hands. It wasn't right to snap at Deidre. It wasn't her fault. "Sorry."

"I get it. It's fine. Do you love her?"

"Yeah, unfortunately I do."

"Why unfortunately? You're not trying to tell me she doesn't love you back."

He lifted a shoulder. "She says she does, but she and I seem to have different ideas about what that means. I'll get over it."

"Oh, Matt. Don't do that. Talk to her."

"Hard to do when she's not here. Look, it's fine, okay?"

Deidre pressed her lips together and shook her head. "You're still coming tonight for game night, and for Christmas, right?"

"I thought I'd spend tonight on the Stingray. There's probably some fine-tuning that still needs to be done. And I haven't decided about Christmas yet. I thought I'd just hang at home and watch some movies."

"Absolutely not. At least come for Christmas Dinner. My folks are coming down and Anna's folks are going to be in from California. Jeremiah's parents are going to be there are well. Danny's spending the day with his family, so there won't be quite as much tension in the air."

He frowned. "Why would Danny cause tension?"

"Never mind. Point being, it's going to be a good time with your friends and lots of food, so you need to be there."

"We'll see. You know what, maybe I'll look into booking a last-minute room and go skiing."

"We haven't had any snow yet. Cold rain, sure, but—"

"They make snow on the ski hills, you know that." Matt shrugged and reached for the new jar of cream. He cracked open the lid and dipped a finger in the cream before working it into his skin. "Seems like it might be a good idea to get away."

"You remember your best friend is getting married three days after Christmas, right?"

"I'm not likely to forget that. I'll be back."

"You better be." Deidre started to say something then shook her head. "The door's open if you change your mind. You don't have to be alone unless it's what you want."

Matt barely managed to keep from rolling his eyes as Deidre stalked out of the garage. Like he had any choice in any of this. He didn't want to be alone. He never had. It was other people who continued to make that choice for him. Why was he suddenly being chastised like he was some kind of sulking toddler for simply deciding to embrace it?

He switched from the radio to a streaming playlist that was heavy on angry rock and roll. Might as well let the music match his mood, maybe it'd help him work out the feelings that crawled up his throat and threatened to spew.

Changing out tools, he was about to slide back under the car when a truck towing a flatbed with a completely covered car pulled into the parking lot. With a sigh, Matt flicked off the music and strode out to the front of his shop.

"Can I help you?"

The man in the passenger seat of the truck flashed a grin. "I hope so. I'm looking for Matt Patterson."

"You found him. What can I do for you?"

The driver turned off the engine and pushed open the door while the passenger hopped out and circled around the front of the truck.

"Greg Schwartz, nice to meet you." The man extended his hand.

Matt took it and eyed the fancy suit the man wore. "How can I help you?"

"I heard you restored a beauty of a 'Vette."

Matt smiled. "Me and my uncle, but yeah. I don't keep it here though, and she's not for sale."

"No. Sorry, you misunderstand. Jerry?" Greg turned and nodded to the man who'd been driving.

Jerry whipped the cover off the car on the flat bed.

Matt's eyebrows lifted. "Is that a 1970 Porsche 911?"

Greg laughed. "Yeah. I know she's in rough shape, but I got her for a song."

"I'm surprised they didn't pay you to take it off their hands." Matt winced. "Sorry."

"Don't worry about it. Close enough. Anyway, this was my dream car growing up and I'm just not willing to pay what they're asking for something in better shape. You think you could get her back to her former glory?"

Matt walked around the trailer eyeing the car. There was a lot of work there. "It's doable. But I can't promise you it won't end up costing more than if you'd just bought one that already worked."

"What are you thinking for labor hourly?" Matt named his usual labor fee and Greg laughed. "That's it?"

"It's what we charge. Small town, right?"

Greg grinned. "Are you interested?"

Matt climbed up on the trailer, reached in through the open—missing?—driver's side window and released the hood. He opened it and peered in. Yeah, it was going to be a lot of work, and not all just on the body. Still, this was a slow time of year.

"If it helps at all, I know a couple of guys who are talking about doing something similar. They see the job you do for me, I can send 'em your way."

That was tempting. Was it a potential sideline for the garage? Something that would keep the money flowing in when things were slow. "Did you have a timeline in mind?"

"Nope. I mean, I'd rather it wasn't years and years, but whatever you think is reasonable and can fit in with your usual workload. Six months? Nine?"

Matt shut the hood and ran a hand over it. "Probably closer to nine. But yeah, I'd like to give it a whirl."

"That's awesome, man. Thanks." Greg grinned and shot Jerry two thumbs up.

Jerry worked some levers and the flatbed began to tilt.

Matt jerked his head toward the office. "Let's go in and write up some paper."

"Makes the world go round, doesn't it?" Greg rubbed his hands together. "I can't wait."

Matt chuckled and held the door. He could probably do the standard paperwork, just without a firm estimate. The longer he thought about it, the more he looked forward to getting started. He ought to be able to finish up his current client's car by this afternoon. Maybe he'd just dig in on the Porsche this weekend instead of going skiing. Always better to make some money than spend it.

And maybe being up to his elbows in an engine would get his mind off his breaking heart.

19

Azure ran a hand over her skirt and took a deep breath. The little Christmas party at the gallery on Friday had gone well. It had been good to meet people who enjoyed her work and have Rob and Crystal introducing her around, but the smaller gathering tonight for Christmas Eve at their house had tied her stomach into knots.

Christmas Eve—and Christmas, for that matter—with complete strangers was odd. Usually, she met up with her parents or at least one of her siblings. Should she have gone back to Arizona to be with them? Maybe Matt would've understood that a little better. She frowned. He didn't seem pre-disposed to understand anything, so probably not. She pushed thoughts of Matt aside, there were enough nerve-wracking things on tonight's agenda without having to worry about the man who said he loved her but clearly didn't understand her at all.

She hushed the little voice that asked if he couldn't say the same thing about her. She'd needed to come for her career as an artist. Matt said he was proud of her talent. If he wasn't just saying that, wouldn't he have understood the importance of that meeting? And this Christmas party?

Enough. She took another deep breath and headed out of her little trailer, across the driveway, and knocked on Rob and Crystal's back door.

"Don't you look nice." Rob pushed open the door with a grin. "Come on in. You're early."

"Too early? Crystal said to come whenever. I thought maybe I could help with something?"

He shook his head. "Crystal's been set for about twenty minutes. She's always early, too. All things considered, it's probably a better habit to have than continuously being late, but don't tell her I said that."

"I heard you anyway." Crystal winked and kissed Rob's cheek. "Come on in and sit in the living room. Tonight's much less formal than the party at the gallery, though some of the people will be the same. We've cultivated a lot of clients from our church."

"And we've introduced other clients to our church and they've ended up staying. It's a lovely thing to be able to serve the Lord and promote art at the same time." Rob chuckled and walked toward the kitchen island where an array of beverages, glasses, and ice were arranged. "Can I get you a drink before you go sit?"

"I'm good, thanks."

"I'd love sparkling water, hon. Come on, Azure, let's go relax until the guests start to arrive. You said you were back at that lovely mansion in Virginia—what was its name again?"

"Peacock Hill." Azure followed Crystal's tall, elegant form to the living room. Extra chairs had been placed around the room and quiet Christmas carols played in the background. "I went back around Thanksgiving. I thought—I met someone when I was there in September. I thought he might be the one."

Crystal's eyebrows rose. "Oh, that's lovely. Tell me all about him."

Pictures of Matt flicked through her head like an old-fashioned movie. She moistened her lips. "I'm not sure I was right about it."

"Hmm. Tell me about him anyway." Crystal settled on one of the straight backed chairs that had clearly been brought in from the dining room and motioned for Azure to take the sofa. "Then you can tell me why you'd say that when I look at you and see a woman in love."

"I didn't say I didn't love him." Azure managed a weak smile. Since Crystal clearly wasn't going to let Azure off the hook, she talked about her contract work at Peacock Hill, meeting Matt, and the pieces of what could pass for their relationship to date. She wound her fingers together in her lap. "So yes, I'm in love with him, but if he doesn't accept who I am, I don't see how there's a future for us."

Crystal nodded. "It's important, certainly, for spouses to understand and accept one another. Have you looked at it from his perspective?"

Azure blew out a breath. "I've tried, but I can't make something rational out of it."

"Can I try?" Rob leaned forward in his chair, elbows on his knees. "As a man, I might have a little bit of an idea what's going through his brain."

Azure snorted. She was pretty certain there was big, stubborn rock in Matt's head where his brain ought to be. "Sure. Why not?"

"You said he's been raised by his aunt and uncle. Where are his parents?"

"They passed away when he was young."

Rob nodded. "And his aunt and uncle just retired and packed off on grand adventures?"

"Right."

"He have any other family?"

"I don't think so." Azure frowned, where was this going? "Although, he has a big group of friends who are almost like family. They spend all their free time in one another's pockets."

Crystal smiled. "You don't like them?"

"Oh, I do. It's just a lot of togetherness. I've spent most of my adult life on my own either driving from one place to another or set up in my trailer."

Rob cleared his throat. "So he's alone, except for his friends, for the first time at Christmas. And he was excited that you were back in town?"

Azure grinned in spite of herself. "Over the moon."

"And then you left him, too." Rob voice was quiet, as if to soften the words. "Do you really not understand why he's upset?"

"I didn't leave. I mean, of course I left, I'm here, but it's not like I abandoned him. I'll go back." Even as she said the words, Azure questioned them. Sure, she intended to go back, but she wasn't committed to staying. Not really. She hadn't even unpacked into the dresser in her room at Peacock Hill. She closed her eyes and reached for the only possible excuse. "You made it seem like it was critical for me to be here."

"Oh, Azure." Crystal shook her head. "You could have told us no. We have little parties at the gallery every couple of months. Neither of us realized you had other plans. We would never have expected you to cancel them just for this. We're used to thinking of you as our gypsy artist, not someone with loved ones to take into consideration."

"I'm not—" Had she really been the one to mess this up so completely?

"He didn't want to tag along?" Rob reached for his wife's water and took a sip, chuckling when she swatted his arm.

"I didn't ask." Azure sighed. "It never even occurred to me."

The doorbell rang and Crystal rose to answer it. She gave Azure a sympathetic squeeze on her shoulder as she passed.

"You okay?" Rob moved to sit beside Azure.

"Other than realizing I'm an idiot? Yeah, I'm fine."

"He'll forgive you. If he loves you and you apologize? He's going to forgive you."

Azure swallowed and fought the tears that wanted to fill her eyes. "I hope so."

After dinner on Christmas day, Azure excused herself and settled on the bed in her trailer. She flipped open her laptop and hooked up to Rob and Crystal's wifi. Her conversation with them before their party the night before had kept her up for a lot of the night alternating between praying and worrying. The worrying hadn't been particularly productive, but the prayers had given her the glimmer of an idea. Or, at least, she figured it was the praying, because the idea that resulted wasn't something she would've come up with on her own.

Now, logging into her email, Azure could only put the credit fully at God's feet again. She ticked through the handful of replies to her online advertisement and considered. She rubbed her chest, trying to ease the twinge in her heart. This was right. It was what she needed to do.

After a few more minutes comparing and looking at maps online, she sent off several emails and sighed. She wanted to talk to Matt. He hadn't called her. Or texted. It wasn't as if she'd reached out, either, but she'd hoped he might be the one to break the ice. He was probably wishing the same thing.

She reached for her phone and opened a new text message. No. She shouldn't be a chicken, no matter how tempting that was. With a quick prayer that he'd answer—and listen—she tapped his photo and waited while it rang.

"Hi."

Azure winced at the brusque greeting and forced a little extra cheer into her voice. "Merry Christmas."

"Yeah. Same to you."

She closed her eyes. No follow on questions, no warmth, even, in his voice. Was she just supposed to be grateful he answered? "I'm sorry, Matt."

"For what? You're just being you, right? I'd assumed you coming back to Virginia and talking about putting down roots meant something different than what you had in mind. It's just good we figured that out now instead of later."

Everything in her froze. He was talking as if they were over. Beyond over. A tear slipped down her cheek. This couldn't be happening. "No, that's not what happened. I do want to put down roots in Virginia. With you. I—I didn't think, and I know that's not a great reason, nor is it an excuse, but I need you to understand that I'm not used to asking permission and thinking about how what I do impacts someone else. I need—want—to change that. I know I hurt you. I'm hoping you can forgive me."

A hint of music and the clink of tools was the only noise on the line for long enough that Azure's stomach began to twist into knots. "Are you there?"

"I am. I'm not sure what you want me to say. I can forgive you, that's no problem, but—"

"Please, can you stop there? I love you, Matt." Azure held her breath and waited with her heart pounding. It couldn't be too late, could it? *Please, Jesus.*

He sighed. Azure could almost picture him running a hand through his hair. "I love you, too, but I'm not sure it's smart."

Some of the tension in her chest eased. It was a place to start. "It's right."

"I guess. I spent the last several days praying for God to take away the feelings I have for you. That didn't work so well."

Now Azure could smile. "I'm awfully glad."

The music clicked off and rustling crackled the line. "How was the party?"

"It would've been better if you'd come with me, but, business-wise, it's good I came. I wish I could rewind and handle it differently though."

"I'm glad it was a success. If you come back this way, I think you'll enjoy the car someone dropped off for me to restore."

"What do you mean if? I'll be home in two days." Home? She hadn't thought about calling it that, but it was the right word. She nodded, rolling the word around in her mind. It was good. Right. Warm. Home.

"That'll make Deidre happy. She keeps asking me when you'll be back. I guess you told her you'd be back for the wedding?"

"I did. Because I will be. And I have our gift for them still, too, though Rob kept trying to buy it."

"Yeah, I thought about that after you stormed off."

She winced. That's not quite how she'd classify how that went down but, it was probably accurate. "Do I need to apologize again?"

"No. I'm sorry. I know I'm easy to leave."

So. Rob was right. "No, you aren't."

Matt snorted.

"It's okay if you don't believe me right now, I get it. But I promise you, you're wrong. I'll prove it when I get back. For now, why don't you tell me about this car and why I'm going to love it?" Had he forgotten she wasn't a gearhead? Not that she minded hearing about cars. Not at all. Especially if it helped them make progress back toward the easy conversation they shared before she proved she was an idiot and came to Atlanta.

Azure settled back against the pile of pillows on her bed and let Matt's voice ease the pockets of pain that still lingered in her heart.

20

Matt glanced out the door of the garage waiting room at the rain. It wasn't quite sleet, but it sure wasn't the same thing as rain in the spring and summer. The roads were already getting slick and it had only been going about an hour. He wasn't likely to get any new business today, and the two oil change appointments he'd had had already cancelled.

Since those two cars belonged to a couple of octogenarians, he didn't begrudge them the rescheduling. He'd get a chance to have a cup of coffee and watch their chess match next week, if the weather held.

Matt smiled and carried his mug over to the coffee maker to refill it. He was still waiting on a part for a transmission repair. It was supposed to come today. At this point, that'd depend on the delivery truck making it up the hills in the area. For now, he'd tinker with the 911 and keep an ear out for tow truck calls. With the roads like they were, that seemed more likely than anything else.

The bell over the door jingled and Jeremiah stomped in, shaking the rain off his jacket. "Gosh it's cold."

"Yeah. That's why they call it winter."

"Yeah, yeah. At least I'll be on a sunny Caribbean beach in two days. They'll still call it winter, but it won't be nearly as miserable."

He had a point. Matt smiled. "Coffee?"

"That'd be great."

"What brings you here the day before your wedding? Checking up on me?"

"Do I need to?" Jeremiah reached for the mug and sipped. "That hits the spot. I thought garages were supposed to have terrible coffee, like police stations."

"Not when the mechanic has to drink it to, they don't. And no, I don't think I need checking up on. My tux is hanging up at my house. The ring is already in the front pocket of the jacket. And I probably have enough entertaining stories about you to make more than one hilarious toast at the rehearsal dinner tonight." Matt took a long drink from his own mug. "So, I'll repeat the question. Not that it's not nice to see you."

"Deidre said I needed to check on you, make sure you were okay."

Matt made the sound of a whip cracking.

Jeremiah shook his head. "Har har. Going to attempt to deflect again?"

"No. I'm good."

Jeremiah just looked at him.

"What?"

"I'm not allowed to accept that answer. Seriously, she'll beat me up if that's all I can give her. She's small, but she's fierce."

"And yet you're marrying her."

"Yeah, well, I adore her." Jeremiah grinned. "Come on, give me something a woman's going to be okay with. Pretend you're on a talk show."

Matt made a gagging motion. "Fine. Look, we talked on Christmas—"

"I probably wouldn't be having this conversation with you if you'd come to Christmas dinner, by the way."

"Right. Because I would have had to have it with Deidre in front of all the parents gathered there. That would've been *so* much better."

"That's a point. Keep going, you talked on Christmas. And?"

Matt sank to the arm of one of the waiting room chairs and stared into his nearly empty mug. And what? They'd talked. Cleared the air, sort of? It didn't change that she'd left without even thinking about how it would come across to him. Sure, she got that now, but how long was it going to take for her to realize that, if he was part of her life, she needed to include him? "We talked. She said she'd be here for the wedding."

"You know that's not what either of us care about, right?"

Matt set his coffee aside. "I know. I don't know what else to say though."

"Do you love her?"

"Unfortunately."

Jeremiah snickered. "Does she love you?"

"She says she does."

"You understand that's really rude, right? If she says she does, then you need to take her word. Let's try again. Does she love you?"

"Fine. Yes."

Jeremiah brightened. "Great. That's what I needed to know. Or Deidre did. You've talked and you're still in love and she'll be back for the wedding."

"I...don't know that I'd sum it up quite like that."

"You're not the one doing it, so it doesn't matter. This'll make Dee happy and that's what I'm going for." Jeremiah drained his coffee and set the empty mug down beside the coffee maker. "See you tonight. Six sharp."

"What if it doesn't work out? How do I know she's not going to leave again?"

Jeremiah tucked his hands in his pockets and fixed Matt in his gaze. "You don't. But you know what Paul says about love in First Corinthians? Love hopes all things, believes all things, and endures all things. It might not be a guarantee, but if you love her, you need to trust her, too. Six o'clock."

"I'll be there." Matt waved.

Hopes all things. What did that even mean? He was going to hope she wouldn't leave again? He already did. But he'd certainly hoped he'd grow up with his mom and dad and that his aunt and uncle wouldn't desert him to go wander the world. Look how well those had turned out.

Okay, it was different. Sort of. But not *that* different.

Trust her.

In a lot of ways, it was easier to love Azure than to trust her. But he wanted to do both.

Matt checked the time on his phone and blew out a breath. It was time to pack it in and get ready for the rehearsal dinner tonight. No sign of Azure yet. He'd expected her to swing by the garage. It wasn't that she'd said she would, but if her whole plan was to come back to him, wouldn't it make sense to come say hi? Maybe she wasn't back in town yet. In which case, she was going to be cutting it close to make the rehearsal dinner. She didn't have to be at the actual rehearsal, but since she lived at Peacock Hill, she was invited. And expected.

He stowed his tools and double-checked that everything was off, closed, and locked before dashing out to his car. The rain had lessened, but it was still a steady sprinkle of cold that managed to find its way down his collar.

Once he was buckled, he started the car and frowned. Fine. He'd call and check in. It wasn't nagging. Or stalking. Or anything like that. He was just making sure she was safe. And still coming. He connected his phone to the stereo and dialed before shifting into gear and heading home.

"Matt? Hi. I was just going to call you."

Sure she was. He frowned. *Believes all things. Yeah, yeah, okay.* "You almost home?"

"Maybe thirty? The rain has been bad and I didn't want to risk an accident, so I've been keeping it just at, maybe a little below, the speed limit."

That was reasonable. Smart, even. Why couldn't she have called and told him that earlier? "Good plan. I can't wait to see you."

"Really? That makes me so happy. I didn't get the feeling that was the case when we talked two days ago."

He winced and turned into the little slide that started when his truck hit an icy patch. "I know. I'm sorry. I'm trying to get over being upset."

Azure was silent for several seconds. "I'm really sorry. If I could go back in time—"

Matt laughed, interrupting her. "I'm not convinced time travel is everything it's cracked up to be. Haven't you seen the TV shows where the whole space-time continuum gets messed up and people cease to exist? I'd just as soon not take that chance. Even if it meant we didn't have a fight."

She chuckled. "All right. If you're sure."

"In this case, I am." He slowed and stopped at the corner before turning onto his street. "That said, could you do me one favor?"

"Absolutely."

"You don't know what it is yet."

"I'll still do it if I can."

If she could. It was a good hedge, as hedges went. "I think it's something you *can* do."

"All right. What is it?"

He took a deep breath. It sounded foolish in his head, but it still got to the core of his pain. If he was going to trust her with his heart, he had to trust her with his hurt. "Next time we fight—cause I'm sure there'll be a next time, we're human—don't leave. Stay and fight."

"I can do that. Do I need to apologize again?"

"No. We're okay. You're going to make it to dinner?"

"I should."

"Then I'll see you there." He shifted into park and stared up at his apartment. "I love you."

"Love you too. I'll see you soon."

He ended the call and blew out a breath. They'd be okay. He could hope, believe, and endure for her. But right this very minute, he needed to shower and change so the best man wasn't late for the rehearsal. He was pretty sure that even as laid back as Deidre had been about the wedding to this point, a late best man wasn't going to go over very well.

21

Azure lingered in her room at Peacock Hill while the sound of wedding rehearsal echoed up to the second floor. Deidre had said to come down whenever, but Azure had wanted a long shower after the drive here. Since it sounded like they were nearly finished, hanging out a little longer was just as easy as going down and interrupting. That would only delay the finish. And dinner.

Her stomach rumbled.

She *definitely* didn't want to delay dinner.

She looked longingly at the overalls she'd painted snowflakes all over that sat on the top of her suitcase and sighed. The dress pants and cheery red sweater were the better choice. She could be comfortable later. Part of her almost wished she had a dress or at least a less-casual skirt than the single denim one she owned. Seeing Matt again mattered. She needed him to know how much she loved him. How serious she was about their relationship. Somehow, it felt like what she wore mattered just as much as anything she could say.

Which clearly meant she was overanalyzing everything.

Honestly. Clothes were clothes. Their whole purpose was to keep people warm and avoid socially awkward nudity. Matt wasn't going to care what she wore.

She pressed a hand to her belly to stop it jumping. The realization that she'd nearly lost him still haunted her dreams. It'd been a week since she stormed off. She'd known then that she loved him, but she'd needed that time apart for her heart to get realigned. A couple was two. Sharing and working together mattered more than her independence. It mattered more than getting her way and doing her own thing. Love mattered more than that. *Matt* mattered more than that.

The sounds from downstairs changed to the quiet rumble of conversation. Azure checked the time. Only ten minutes past when Deidre had thought they'd be done. Close enough. With a steadying breath, she slipped into her dressy flats and skipped down the stairs.

Her gaze scanned the small crowd until she spied Matt. Her mouth went dry. There he was. He looked amazing in crisply pleated khakis and a navy cable-knit sweater. He was laughing with Jeremiah. Love swelled in her chest. Azure took the last stair and crossed the foyer, her gaze steady on Matt.

"Hi."

He turned and a slow smile spread across his face, his eyes lighting. "There you are."

Azure flung her arms around him and breathed in his scent. Home. This, right here, was home.

"I'll just leave you two alone and go see if Deidre needs any help getting the catering set up." Jeremiah chuckled and punched Matt in the shoulder. "Glad you made it, Azure."

She stepped back. "Sorry."

"You need to stop saying that." Matt brushed his lips across hers.

Azure reached up and pulled his mouth back to hers, pouring herself into the kiss and letting the little sparks of electricity caress her skin.

Matt leaned back, a smile flirting with the corners of his lips. "Well. Hi."

"You said that already." She leaned her head on his shoulder. "I missed you."

"Yeah? Me, too. I didn't see your trailer outside, you park it in the back?"

Azure hesitated. This wasn't quite where she'd planned to have that conversation. Still, he asked. "No, I—"

"Everyone? If you'd all like to come to the dining room, dinner's ready." Jeremiah's voice projected well enough that conversations quieted and the group began to mill toward the food.

Matt slid his hand down Azure's arm and clasped her hand. "Come on, we can talk at dinner. Did I say I was glad you're back?"

"No. It's good to hear." She breathed in the scent of dinner. "Smells amazing."

"Taco bar. Or you can do nachos. Nachos are kind of Jeremiah's thing, so this is right up his alley. Of course, I don't think it's possible for anyone to do nachos like he does them, but he says this place is almost as good." Matt led Azure to the end of the line that had formed where the buffet was set up.

Azure scanned the people. She recognized most of the faces from her time at Peacock Hill. Duncan and Anna, an older couple who bore enough of a resemblance to Duncan and Deidre that they had to be their parents, Claire, Danny, and Mr. and Mrs. Crawford, who she'd met a couple of times at church. The pastor was there with his wife, and a handful of others from church that she recognized but couldn't place.

They inched their way toward the food. Matt kept her hand in his, almost as if he was scared to let go lest she disappear. She squeezed his fingers. "I'm not going anywhere."

"I believe you." He brushed his lips across her forehead.

She warmed all the way through, his forgiveness and love a sweet balm.

When dinner was finished and all the funny stories from Deidre and Jeremiah's childhood had been told, Matt and Azure helped to clear away the debris. The food had been packaged up and sent home with guests.

All that remained was to sweep and do some rudimentary setup for the reception the next day.

"We've got this. Why don't the two of you go for a walk?" Mrs. Crawford patted Matt on the arm. "Wear a hat though, it's cold."

Cold and, if it was like the rest of the day, rainy. She glanced at Matt and whispered, "Did the rain stop?"

He nodded and led her out of earshot. "We don't have to walk if you don't want to. It's probably slick still. Have you been up in the towers?"

She frowned. There was the stone tower at the back of the property. But that couldn't be what he meant if he wasn't dragging her outside. There were towers on either side of the main house, but she'd assumed they were ornamental, not something that could be reached. "No. I don't think so."

"Let's do that, then. They're still open at the top, but they have a roof and fairly high walls, so it shouldn't be too cold. Do you want to grab your coat on the way up?"

"Yeah. If you don't mind."

"Course not." He grinned and held out his hand. "Shall we?"

She slipped her fingers into his and they climbed the main staircase, pausing to admire the stained glass at the landing. It was so pretty. Everything here was. Deidre had found a gem when she'd purchased this place.

At the second floor landing, Azure hurried to her room to snag her coat. She was slipping into the sleeves as she rejoined Matt. "Okay, now where?"

"The side stairs." Matt tugged toward the end of the hall. "They lead up to the third floor and, from there, you can access the towers."

"Ah. That explains it. I was told the third floor was for the men."

Matt laughed. "Yeah, Duncan has a couple of rooms up here and when Sean's stayed over, he's up here too. Probably just as well you didn't go exploring. Here, we head down this little hall and through the door and—"

The blast of cold air stole Azure's breath. "Oh wow. Cold."

"Too cold?"

She zipped up her jacket. "No. I'll be okay. Now I want to see it."

With a grin, Matt led her through a tiny room to a skinny set of stairs that led up another story and ended in the top of a tower. The space was probably ten feet square with openings on all sides giving views that had to be spectacular in the daytime.

"I'd love to paint up here. In the summer."

Matt moved to stand behind her and wrapped his arms around her waist. "Better?"

She relaxed into his warmth and let her head rest against his shoulder. "Much."

"I don't see your trailer in back, either."

"I sold it."

Matt's body twitched, his arms tightening around her. "What?"

"It's why I couldn't get back until today. I had to detour to the Florida state line to meet the buyer. They're turning it into a little rental in their back yard. I guess they have a place right on the gulf coast, so renters can walk to the beach." Azure turned in his embrace and slid her arms around his waist, tilting her head up so she could meet his gaze. "I wanted you to understand I'm serious about staying here and putting down roots. With you."

Matt lowered his forehead to hers.

"So you see, I won't be running off the next time we fight, because my home isn't something I can hook to my truck and pull wherever I want. My home is where you are. I've never wanted to run away from home."

"I love you."

She smiled and cradled his cheek. "Are you going to marry me?"

He blinked. "Am I...really? Do I get a ring?"

Azure chuckled. "No. You still have to do that part. And ask me properly."

"I don't know. I kind of like that you asked me."

"Matt."

"What?"

She frowned and looked away. She hadn't meant to ask that, and now he wasn't answering. Had she miscalculated that badly? Jumped too fast? Should she back pedal?

"Azure?"

She turned back and met Matt's gaze.

"Will you marry me?"

Everything in her loosened and her eyes filled. She swallowed and nodded.

"A nod? That's it?"

She chuckled. "No."

His face fell. "No?"

"No. No that's not all. Not no. Yes." She laughed and buried her face in his shoulder for a moment. How had this gone so terribly wrong? When she was back under control, she looked up and held Matt's gaze. "Yes, I'll marry you. I love you."

He lowered his mouth to hers. "Welcome home."

Want a free book?

If you enjoyed *A Heart Realigned* and would like to read another book of mine, you can receive a free novel, simply by signing up for my newsletter here: http://bit.ly/2g0AGvf

Look for *A Heart Redirected*, book 4 in the Peacock Hill Romance series, coming soon!

Author's Note

Thank you for reading *A Heart Realigned!* I hope that you enjoyed getting to know Matt and Azure. I would appreciate it if you'd help others enjoy it too by leaving a review and telling your friends about it. Any success my books have is owed to readers like you who take the time to tell others about my stories. Thank you, from the bottom of my heart. I hope you'll continue to join me in exploring Peacock Hill, that lovely old house in the mountains.

I continue to owe a huge debt of gratitude to my husband and sons for giving me the time to write, my sister for her unflinching support and encouragement, and my critique partners Heather Gray, Jan Elder, and Valerie Comer. More than anything, I'm grateful that God continues to give me words and makes it possible for me to write them down.

I'd love to hear from you! You can connect with me on Facebook

(www.Facebook.com/ElizabethMaddrey)

my webpage (www.ElizabethMaddrey.com) or via email. To stay current with news and occasional giveaways, please subscribe to my newsletter (links on Facebook or my webpage).

About the Author

Elizabeth Maddrey began writing stories as soon as she could form the letters properly and has never looked back. Though her practical nature and love of computers, math, and organization steered her into computer science at Wheaton College, she always had one or more stories in progress to occupy her free time. This continued through a Master's program in Software Engineering, several years in the computer industry, teaching programming at the college level, and a Ph.D. in Computer Technology in Education. When she isn't writing, Elizabeth is a voracious consumer of books and has mastered the art of reading while undertaking just about any other activity.

Elizabeth is the author of more than ten books, both fiction and non-fiction. She lives in the suburbs of Washington, D.C. with her husband and their two incredibly active little boys.